DEFIANT DEVOTION

LEONA WHITE

Copyright © 2025 by Leona White

All rights reserved.

No part of this book may be reproduced in any form or by any electronic or mechanical means, including information storage and retrieval systems, without written permission from the author, except for the use of brief quotations in a book review.

❦ Created with Vellum

ALSO BY LEONA WHITE

Mafia Bosses Series

The Irish Arrangement || The Last Vendetta

The Constella Family

Under His Protection || Under His Watch || Under His Control || Under His Embrace

The Baranov Legacy

Guarded Rebellion || Savage Surrender || Shielded Secrets || Defiant Devotion

LEONA WHITE

Holiday Mafia Standalone's

Velvet Deception ‖ Twin Deception

BLURB

I'm paid to kill, not to care.

One night with a mysterious woman in a small town haunted my dreams.

Then I found her again – the lost Baranov princess.

Carrying my child, running from demons I was hired to protect.

She's thirteen years younger, *innocent despite her darkness.*

The virgin sacrifice in a mafia war I never wanted to join.

But now her enemies are mine to destroy.

They think they can use her as a pawn? *I'll burn their empire to ashes.*

The hitman without a home has found something worth dying for.

Her defiance awakens my devotion.

And I'll paint this city red to keep what's mine.

Author's Note: *Defiant Devotion* features a protective alpha male, age gap romance, and forced proximity. Contains dark mafia themes, steamy scenes, and pregnancy. This standalone romance in The Baranov Legacy series guarantees an HEA.

1

SONYA

The last time I tried to break out of this house was during the coldest weeks of winter. Almost a year ago, at the end of January, the snow gave me away. My footprints were too traceable in my route from this damn farmhouse I'd been held captive in for the last eleven years. Blizzard-like conditions were supposed to have been my cover, both to mask my path and to prohibit any of these thugs from chasing me down.

They always did. Every time. Without fail, these Ilyin assholes would find me and drag me back into the room I was supposed to wait and live in until they deemed I was "ready".

The snow foiled my last grand plans to get the fuck out of here. It hadn't mattered how quickly I ran and darted behind structures coated with thick snow. They'd found me.

That time, I almost reached the second fence to scale it to flee.

This time...

I paused at the fence and glanced back over my shoulder, glad that in this last week of February no snow was blanketing the landscape on this night. No white fluff to indicate where I'd placed my feet. No winds to send my long brown hair flowing out of my hood and giving away my location.

No guards or patrolmen noticing my attempt to bolt.

Only the navy-blue darkness of the starless sky hung overhead. Shadows concealed me in this pitch blackness.

Go. Stop stalling and just go!

I wouldn't have another chance. Driven not only by the need to survive and escape this captivity, but I was also motivated with the urgency to thwart those bastards' plans.

For eleven damn years, I'd been held here upstate and cut off from the rest of the world. For over a decade, I had to accept that the Ilyins wanted to stoop so low as to kidnap a Mafia princess like me just to marry me off when they deemed the timing to be right.

And that time was now. Yesterday, I eavesdropped and listened in to the guards talking about finally being done with keeping me up here. That I would be sent off to my "fiancé" within the week. That I'd be shipped away and expected to serve as a pawn in a dangerous political game.

"Fuck that," I muttered under my breath. The mere notion of being used as a virginal transaction lit a fire within me. Despite the bite of the chill in the wintry air, I felt as though I was burning up from the inside out.

With rage. Fury. Anger born of the darkest wrath. I harbored all three.

I hated my captors for taking me. I loathed those same Mafia men for raping my mother and killing her before my eyes. I scorned them for distancing me from my family.

And I dared them to steal anything else from me.

As I ran again, careful to slip under the eyeline of the patrolmen who'd hawk around the perimeter fence of the property, I let that fiery thought be my mantra.

I'll be damned if you use me.

I'll be goddamned if you try to rob my virginity as a power play.

Pumping my arms, I dug my feet in faster and harder after climbing the second fence. I wasn't escaping under any illusion that I'd succeed, not with my freedom. I would never be free. In each of my five attempts to get away from these men who'd kidnapped me so many years ago, I learned and relearned the cruel lesson that there were simply too many loyalists and fearful men in this small town for me to ever actually leave. All my previous attempts to flee ended the same. I had been dragged back, beaten, and expected to stay put. Again.

This time would be different.

This time, I would not be returned in defeat.

I *would* be married to whoever they wanted to force me to be with. I knew that. They outnumbered me and were in control here.

But I would not be a virginal bride when they found me again.

I wouldn't let them steal that one thing they had no business even concerning themselves with.

Instead of running my breath ragged as I sprinted toward the main street of the small town with an intention to disappear, I focused on accomplishing the ultimate twist. I concentrated on how I could mess up their grand plan to offer me as a virginal bride to someone I didn't know, much less want.

"Whoa!" a man said as he exited the small bar at the end of the main street.

I hadn't been granted many chances to see this town, but over the last eleven years, I'd pieced together small snippets of this rural area to have a halfway decent mental map in my head. The bar, just like the guards often said, was right at the end of the street, near the property I had been held at. And exactly like the guards said, it was often dark, full of smoke, and narrow.

"Sorry," I muttered to whoever I'd crashed into with my rush to enter the tiny establishment. I wasn't sorry. I didn't give a shit who I knocked into. I was on a mission to fuck the first man I saw, and nothing else mattered. Yet, I halfheartedly apologized to the old senior as he used his cane to lumber out of the bar. It was by rote, automatically expected of me just because I was a woman in a man's world. Always just a little "girl" in the big, bad man's world.

Passing him by, I let the cloak of impatience settle over me. I scanned the small bar, checking that none of the occupants were members of the Ilyin force. If I risked running out a week before my engagement would be official, all to be caught by one of the men out here drinking, I'd never forgive myself. That was why I'd chosen this night, though. Why I had decided to attempt this stunt when they were most likely drinking at the guesthouse for one of their habitual, biweekly parties. They never lowered their guard enough for me to be confident about escaping, but if there were ever a chance to sneak out of their sight for a little while, it'd be now.

There. I narrowed my eyes, still catching my breath, and studied the tall, lone man seated at the end of the bar. He was by himself, drinking a beer. But his lack of company wasn't all that made me zero in on him. It was his distance from the others, as though he wanted nothing to do with the other older men in here drinking and bullshitting. Besides him, the clientele were either in groups or coupled with a woman.

It has to be him.

No one else would work, and I couldn't fail.

After I swallowed, annoyed with how dry my mouth was, I lifted my chin and strode directly toward him.

Even though I'd been a resident of the area for eleven years, none of the locals knew me. I was just another random stranger here, one with a clear and needy goal.

I walked too quickly, pretending to trip over my feet just as I neared him. Crashing against his shoulder, I was treated to the first demonstration of how rugged and fit this tall guy was.

Damn.

I was familiar with strong, buff men. All the Baranov guards and soldiers back home were built like this, and the Ilyin assholes here who kept me captive were cut of the same cloth. Mafia men were all the same—strong and fit to incite danger and violence.

Up this close, as he reached out to steady me from my fake fall, he gave me a hint of his scent, that spicy cologne and muskier note of all male. This was a manly man, and I prayed I could dupe him. I hoped he wasn't too experienced and wizened that he wouldn't still fall for my best stab at seduction.

"Oh!" I blinked my eyes, feigning shock as I righted myself. "I didn't mean to…"

"It's all right." He chuckled slightly, and I couldn't help but guess that he made that sound at my expense. That he was laughing *at* me for being so clumsy, not that he was laughing with me at the silly collision.

He had to be one of those serious ones, then. I cringed, worried that might be an obstacle.

I nodded, keeping my gaze down so I could look demure and shy. "I didn't mean to interrupt." Relying on the old memories of my aunt whose favorite pastime had been fucking all the Baranov soldiers and guards at the mansion, I traced the tip of my tongue along my lower lip then set my teeth on it.

He swiveled. Just like that, it worked. Spinning on his stool to fully face me as I stood next to him, he slapped all his attention on me. I'd caught his attention, and now, I had to keep it.

"Interrupt what?" he asked with a lazy shrug of one massive shoulder.

"Your evening," I said softly, smiling a bit to let him think I was naïve and meek. Men liked that, didn't they? They always had to be superior and calling the shots, not just in my life as Mafia men, but all over the world.

"It's been dull," he said, gesturing with his hand for me to sit next to him. "But now that you're here, maybe you can help me liven it up."

Yes. Yes! I couldn't believe that it was working. That merely facing this rugged man with impossibly dark eyes could make this a reality. I'd planned to sneak out and fuck a stranger all to thwart my captors, but not once did I have the confidence that it could work.

"Oh, I can't." I shook my head slightly without stepping back.

Play hard to get. Look shy. Smile sweetly.

I was a virgin, closed off from the world for the last eleven years. I didn't know how to flirt or how to seduce a man. All I had were the memories of my horny cougar of an aunt from long ago.

"No?" He arched a brow, calmly setting his elbow on the top of the bar so he could continue to face me. "You can't or won't?"

I did that shy smile again, giving him a little more rope to think that he was tempting me. "Can't. I really… Well, I really shouldn't."

"Why's that?" he asked. Not nosy. Not pushy. Merely curious.

When I risked another glance at his handsome face, I wondered if that smoldering gaze truly meant he desired me. It felt like it. Under his serious stare, I felt like he was stripping me bare.

"I have something else to do tonight."

"Hmm." He lifted his beer and took a drink, not tearing his gaze off me for a second. The door opened and closed behind me, and I couldn't help but flinch. In the process, I stepped closer to him, that much further between his legs that he parted to let me stand in his space. "And what's that? What does a gorgeous woman like you have planned for the night?"

Here goes. I licked my lip again, then touched my teeth to the corner of it. "I plan to..." Lowering my gaze wasn't an act. It *was* hard to just come out and so bluntly dare to say this.

Hurry up. You have to try. You can't go back and let them take this from you too.

I swallowed hard, took a deep breath, and raised my gaze to his. "I plan to lose my virginity tonight."

He didn't react. Not a flinch. No lift of his brows in surprise. He was a serious guy, all right.

"I want to find someone to sleep with," I said, amazed that my tone was stronger the more I spoke. Something about him relaxed me.

"Someone willing to show me a good time," I clarified. It didn't matter if I enjoyed it. It'd probably hurt having sex for the first time. But it would be my choice to make. My only choice to ever make again before I was some asshole's wife.

Still, he watched me with that stern seriousness. But the longer he didn't reply, the more I worried he would reject such an out-of-the-blue comment like that. Or maybe he knew an Ilyin guard. What if...

"Anyone would do?" he asked at last, his voice so gruff and thick, like the whiskey they might pour here.

I nodded, braving another small step toward him when his gaze darkened with lust. "Any—"

He gripped the front of my coat and pulled me even closer. With the force of his tug, I almost crashed against him again. Stopped when I slammed against his chest, I held my breath at how he'd nearly wrenched me all the way forward until our lips could've touched.

He remained an inch apart from me, his mouth curling up in a slow, mischievous smile at my gasp of surprise. "Anyone?" he asked again. Dragging his hand lower until he snaked his arm around my back, until he hugged me as he studied me, he brushed my hair back and tucked it behind my ear.

Holy shit. How can... How can he be this good? This sexy and... and...

I'd come here desperate to seduce the first man I found. But I hadn't been prepared for a cunning guy like him to turn the tables and make me needy instead.

His touch burned. That steady, deep stare of his unraveled me. It was the soft press of his lips on my cheek that had my pulse racing, though. "Even me?" he whispered against my ear.

Oh, my God.

"Yes," I replied. "Even you."

"A stranger?" he asked.

I nodded, more eagerly. "No names. Just… sex." Slanting into him felt natural. As he reared back to see my face as he talked, I mourned the absence of his warmth.

"This isn't some kind of a prank or something, is it?"

"No. I just want…" I swallowed hard, closing my eyes more under the tender caress of his palm as he cupped my face. "I just want to live my life. To be wild for once."

"Say no more, *stranger*." A devilish grin covered his face as he leaned in to kiss me slowly. Deeply.

It was my first kiss.

My first foray into the dangerous game of desire.

The electric pressure of his hot mouth over mine was over all too soon. In an instant, I craved him to do it again. I craved all he could give me. Wanting his lips on me again, I gasped at the pure need he'd caused me to struggle with so instantly.

"Let's get out of here," he suggested, taking my hand and guiding me to follow him out of the bar.

I opened and closed my mouth, stupefied by the lingering burn of his kiss. Clinging to the hot grip of his strong hand over mine, I tried not to sink under the overwhelming excitement—and slight nervousness—of being led to the one and only time I'd have sex with someone of my choosing.

Just like that, I was about to lose my virginity.

It was a fool's errand when I'd be subjected to whatever my husband demanded of me soon enough. But right now, under this stranger's warm hold on my hand, I felt more alive than I ever had before.

For the first time in eleven years, I was acting out.

I was defiant.

I was rebelling against my captors' wishes.

Finally, after having no control, I'd wrested a little of it back to me.

I wouldn't be some *thing* to barter with. I wouldn't be a pure virgin anymore.

And it would all be worth it.

A small smile teased my lips as the stranger opened the door and led me out into the cold once more.

2

BEN

Current day...

As far as weddings went, this one was fancy. It should've been the wedding of the decade, a marriage for the powerful Baranov family.

All the prominent members of society were here as guests at Oleg Baranov's mansion. The family considered this their "home", and it seemed fitting that they'd host the ceremony uniting Eva Baranov and Lev Kvashnin here. The Mafia princess and her elite bodyguard, married under the big boss's approval.

They'd spared no expenses, of course, and the entire scene was one straight out of a fairytale. Champagne flowed. Live music carried through the ornately decorated ballroom, competing with the din of lively conversations among the Baranov family members and their guests.

Some of those conversations were to do with business. Of course, they were. A gathering of the Baranov Mafia Family would result in discussions about business, particularly with how recently someone had taken a potshot at the top man himself. Oleg Baranov had been shot at, but it seemed like Eva's uncle had not a care in the world as he sat back and celebrated this union.

I knew better. Oleg Baranov hadn't become the Baranov boss idly. He had to be curious about who'd tried to kill him.

I was curious, enough that I snuck in to spy on this event.

Once more, I subtly glanced in the direction of where Rurik Baranov sat at the head table. He was one of the groomsmen, naturally, because he was a cousin to Eva. Yet, I had extra interest in him because he had been the guard who'd saved Oleg's life. When someone shot Oleg Baranov, Rurik had taken the bullet for him.

Who did it, though? Who hired those men to shoot that day?

I wasn't passionate about Oleg living or dying. But since Oleg was the Boss and I had been previously approached by the head of the Baranovs' rival, Igor Petrov, with a hit he wanted to place on his competition, I had to be intrigued.

Ever since I left the military and moved stateside, I'd been known as a hitman with no loyalties. If the price was decent, if I was interested in the challenge, I'd take the assignment. When Igor had come to me back in the beginning of March, asking me to kill Oleg Baranov, I didn't get a good vibe from him about it. Money was money. Sure, it made the world go round. I had more money than I'd ever be able to spend, though, so I could afford this extra consideration. Taking jobs from the three main Mafia Families in this area gave me a unique position of independence, and I wanted to choose wisely when I accepted such a big hit. Killing a Boss was no small murder.

"I'm telling you, Ben's the one to do it."

I tore my gaze away from the direction of the head table where Rurik sat with the new couple. Eva and Lev were the stars of this night, no doubt, but I'd snuck in here undercover and in a disguise for *these* kinds of conversations. The whispered discussions where business was dealt with.

Vik, another Baranov, stood next to me at the bar where I blended in as just another guest among the many. I wasn't sure which soldier he was speaking to, but I was very aware of the matter of their quiet conversation off to the side.

Because they were talking about *me*.

"I'm not arguing that," the Baranov soldier said. "I've heard the same shit about Ben Warner that everyone else has. He's an elite assassin. The best of the best."

I bit back the urge to smile. Pride filled me at this praise I'd eavesdropped on. Being proud of a career was one matter, but taking glee in my ability to always claim a kill was something better that appeased the darkness in my soul.

"But he's also hard to get ahold of," the man added. "And picky about what jobs he takes."

I could've nodded right along. *Damn straight, I'm picky.* I saw no reason not to be when I was playing God, deciding who lived or died. When it came to accepting contracts from the Mafia, I wanted to be careful of whom I was aligning with. Igor Petrov irritated me. The Ilyins were getting on my nerves too. That was why I'd come here tonight, to spy on the Baranovs and really get a better feeling for what kind of men they were.

Lev Kvashnin had started the process of reaching out to me. He'd gone through the proper channels of seeking me out. Like the others, he wanted to hire me for a hit—one placed on the next governor to be sworn in.

It wouldn't be an impossible job, but I needed more details first. I wanted to know more background information so I could determine whether killing someone for the Baranovs was a good use of my time.

A good use of my time?

I resisted the urge to roll my eyes. Working wasn't that much fun anymore. It was harder and harder to achieve that thrill of a difficult kill. The last time I felt like I'd had fun was three months ago when that sexy young woman hit me up at the bar and asked me to help her lose her virginity. I still couldn't get her out of my mind.

"Lev will reach out to him again once the wedding celebrations die down," Vik said. "It's not like we can sit on it for long."

Ignoring the lingering distraction of a thought about that woman, I tuned in to their conversation again.

"Why?" the other man asked. "Because Rurik is impatient to kill O'Malley for Kelly's peace of mind?"

Peace of mind? I wasn't following. That wasn't any reason to put a hit on someone.

I glanced at the woman he'd referenced. Kelly Garnet sat next to Rurik, smiling and seeming at ease. I'd learned that they'd gotten together recently, and while it wasn't unheard of for a man to kill another for his woman, I felt like I needed more intel to piece this together.

I didn't just kill hits. I could start wars. I could impact the economy. I could instigate further danger. Death wasn't some token of fun to dole out. Understanding the potential results of killing O'Malley was imperative.

"Yeah," Vik replied. "O'Malley's gotta go because of the threat he holds over Kelly. She's one of us now."

I filed that information away. It seemed Kelly and Rurik were already married, even though they hadn't done an elaborate wedding like this. Still, I had heard that another Baranov wedding would be coming up, with Irina and Vik being engaged. Love was certainly in the air for this group.

"But rumors are spreading that he's interested in backing one of the families around here. And it wouldn't be us." Vik sighed. "We all know how Oleg views the politicians."

The other man chuckled lightly. "Yeah. He doesn't have any patience for them."

"They're too selfish. Too sneaky and out for themselves," Vik replied.

Aren't you all? That was my opinion of all the damn Mafia organizations around here.

"But—"

"Uncle Oleg!" Eva shot to her feet with that shout. She hadn't only cut off whatever this soldier was going to tell Vik at the bar. Her yell captured the attention of nearly everyone in the ballroom. The music was cut short. Chatter ceased. And with the quiet, we all could actually hear the thud of Boris's body falling to the floor.

Eva's father clutched his chest as he keeled over. Oleg rushed toward his younger brother, flanked by many soldiers. Orders for medical help followed, and as a crowd gathered around the fallen Baranov brother, no doubt drunk again, I failed to see what was happening.

Is he dead? Did someone shoot him? I didn't hear anything go off. What the hell is going on?

It happened so suddenly that I couldn't keep up with the chaotic commotion that followed. Eva must have been watching her father to alert her uncle to his falling over, but now that everyone was trying to get close and handle the situation, I had my chance to slip away.

If Boris was dead, I didn't want to be hanging around here. He was the younger brother, the spare, the useless drunk of the two brothers in this family, but he was still an upper member of the organization. His death would be significant. Furthermore, if he died from something that happened at this wedding, it would be a grave attack on the family.

"Time to go," I muttered under my breath, slipping backward through the crowd of worried guests. My disguise was foolproof. No one would be able to identify me here, but just in case security was heightened even more after Boris's fall, I wanted to be far from the scene.

No one stopped me as I exited, but I remained tense until I was back in my car, ready to drive away.

"What the hell was that about?" I whispered to myself as I started the engine and scanned my surroundings again.

Boris? Who'd want him *dead? He's useless.*

Still, no one came to stop me from leaving. I drove toward the exit, my mind racing a mile a minute with too many questions.

Igor wants Oleg dead, but he never said anything about Boris.

I shook my head as I drove, confused and eager to investigate this from afar.

What started as a night of eavesdropping and spying on the Baranovs turned into witnessing a potential death. And it wasn't something I wanted to be involved in at this moment. If Boris was dead, fingers would be pointed and blame would be placed on someone's shoulders.

Just not mine.

Not this time.

But if someone else was trying to do my work and interfere with the hits I might potentially accept and make my business, something had to be done about that.

3

SONYA

It was time for me to escape. This time, I *had* to. Not just to sneak out and have sex with a stranger. I needed to get the hell out of here and end my captivity once and for all.

Footsteps sounded down the hallway outside my room, and I held my breath.

Ever since I heard the guards talking about transporting me to the city, I freaked out. Last night, two of the loudmouths were arguing about who'd get to drive and where they'd get to go after dropping me off to my fiancé.

"No. It's your turn to drive," one Ilyin guard said with an exasperated sigh as they walked past my locked door. Following the capture after I had sex with that tall, rugged stranger in his motel room, they'd upped the surveillance on me. The Ilyin bastards considered me more of a flight risk, ensuring that patrols passed my door around the clock now.

"I don't care," the guard's companion said just as tiredly. Clearly, they were old partners, used to arguing. "I'm not in the mood to drive for three hours and—"

"But it is your turn," the first one repeated.

Pressing my ear to the door to better listen, I rolled my eyes and wished they'd cut out this damn arguing. Yes, yes. Neither wanted to drive. Both of them were looking forward to leaving this property. One wanted to go straight to a club, and the other was more interested in visiting a whorehouse while they were in the city.

I needed facts. I wanted details about the timing. The location. The vehicle. The more I knew, the better I could plot to get away—for good.

I have to get out of here.

Gulping down a hard swallow, my throat so dry since no one had brought me more water when I requested it, I winced and lowered my hand from the wooden surface of the door to lay it over my stomach.

We *have to get out of here.*

When I planned to thwart the Ilyins by losing my virginity before meeting my fiancé, I hadn't considered the odds that I could end up pregnant.

From just that one interaction, that single, initial act of intimacy, and ta-da, I was pregnant.

Sure, it could happen. It only took once to get knocked up. I *knew* that. It was simple science. One sperm had to find its way to an egg and a baby would follow. One shot was all it took. Yet, the fate of that happening to me, in these circumstances, was twisted.

Evading my forced engagement was a goal. Now with a child growing inside me, though, it had become my mission.

We will get out. Promising my baby seemed foolhardy, but I stood by my wishes. I had to.

I couldn't be handed over already pregnant. It would be too obvious of an indicator that I wasn't the virgin they expected. It would be too clear of evidence to show that something had been reneged or changed in the deal. Offending the people who'd dared to make deals about my future and my life wasn't the issue, but I wasn't naïve. I was well aware that the more this deal seemed botched, the worse I would be punished for it.

"Okay, okay," the guard said as the pair walked by my closed door again. "We'll take her to Benson's place, then head to the club near…"

Their words faded as they strolled further down the hall. But that was fine. I didn't care what they wanted to do after they'd transported me.

That name mattered, though.

Benson?

I scrunched my face, thinking back for the significance. I'd heard of a Benson before, but I had no clue who it was. I couldn't tell if I'd heard the name while I was in captivity here or if it was a moniker that seemed familiar from when I lived at home, with the Baranov family I missed so much.

Benson. Benson. Benson…

This was the first time I'd heard who my fiancé was supposed to be. Having that clue was like light coming in through the shroud of darkness and lack of knowledge they'd kept me in these past eleven years. All that time, I knew I was being held as a virginal bride for *someone* when they deemed the time was right. They'd thought the time was right three months ago. But it was now.

Benson…

I cringed as I concentrated, too frantic to place the name.

Someone from another Mafia family? The Bratva? A gang? The Cartel? Racking my brain didn't help, but I was confident that the man they wanted to force me to marry had to be someone in power. My capture and forced marriage had to be a transaction of some kind, and I knew better than to think this could be a random match that they had in mind for me.

Benson?

No one came to mind, but as the footsteps went by again, I shook my head and scowled. It hardly mattered what my fiancé's name was. It was only important to realize that I'd soon be handed off to him, whoever he was. And he wouldn't be happy to see that I was already knocked up.

"The timing is actually in our favor," one guard gossiped.

"What," his partner replied, "delivering her now instead of back in February?"

"Yeah."

The other man grunted. "Well, if she hadn't acted out and tried to sneak away, we probably would've delivered her then."

No guilt or shame filled me. I wouldn't regret sneaking out and giving away my virginity on my terms. I couldn't regret this baby, either. This new life was giving *me* new life, encouraging me to break out of here once and for all just to protect him or her.

"No, I doubt it. Benson was too busy then. But now, with Boris dying, we'll be done with the Baranovs for good."

My mouth dropped open. With how dry and chapped my lips were, I didn't need to aggravate the lack of moisture. Lip balm wasn't a necessity during imprisonment.

It hung for another moment, too. Shock reverberated through me, holding me in place and barely cognizant of my surroundings.

Boris? Boris Baranov? He's... dead?

Blinking at the thought, I tried to snap out of this stunned status. I couldn't lock down under shock. I couldn't let myself be hindered by a surprise like this.

I had been so limited, so deprived of information about my family that I had to ferret out nuggets of gossip like this.

Overhearing the news that my father was dead threatened to knock me down.

How? Why? How can he be dead too?

Without a phone or computer, I'd been stuck in ignorance for over a decade. No allies got word to us. Nothing at all. That lack of information had been hardest on my mother before they'd killed her, but I learned to pocket scraps of news the guards were too lazy to hide as they talked among themselves. Playing the meek, quiet, shellshocked captive girl allowed me to blend into the background, and they spoke freer around me.

Boris is dead?

This timing was terrible!

"It can't be..." I muttered to myself as I lifted my hand to my mouth. Placing my fingertips over my lips wouldn't block the words from leaving. But I wished I could erase this news.

Boris Baranov was dead, and that meant no leader remained over my family. Oleg was killed not long after Mother and I had been taken. I overheard the Ilyin men bragging about killing my uncle many years ago. All this time, I'd held on to the faith that my father, weak and drunk though he was, would stay strong as the family's patriarch.

Not anymore.

Not now.

Without my father at the helm, my younger sister would be left unguarded. Anyone could force her into marriage. Anyone could try to end my family now. The Baranov legacy, the family name, was vulnerable to be overtaken more than ever.

Panic rose within me. Fear claimed my thoughts as I tried to process this news.

Boris was dead. Oleg and my mother had been killed years ago. No other siblings would be waiting out there.

It was just Eva back home, open to be taken and used.

Just like me.

"No." Tears stung at my closed lids as I squeezed them tight.

I couldn't bear the thought of her suffering like I had.

No!

A sob threatened to break free at the thought of my younger sister suffering. I held it back, though, determined not to let the guards hear me near the door. I had to keep my strong, defiant mask on a little longer, until I got out of here.

It had been years since I'd seen Eva. She would be grown now, ripe for marriage and defenseless to the men who held all the power in our world. But my love for her hadn't ever faded. My devotion to the family hadn't ceased once.

I didn't *know* this baby that grew in my belly, but I was already fiercely protective of wanting to spare him or her from a life with this Benson man I'd marry.

I did know my sister back home, though, and I was equally filled with rage to protect her from being taken without our uncle or father in charge of the family.

This was *it*.

The time had come, and there wouldn't be second chances.

If it was the last thing I did, I had to break out of here and get back to my family.

Keeping my narrowed gaze on the closed door of my locked room, I backed up steadily. Those two men would be coming in here tomorrow to transport me. They'd unlock the hardware, step inside my cell, and approach me to drag me toward my fiancé.

Not happening.

Once more, until I'd have my strategy memorized without error, I retraced my steps and practiced how I could evade them and escape. Over and over, with this burning need to defy them all, I rehearsed how I'd slip the hidden knife out from its hiding place under my mattress. How I'd play dead and feign my submission until one came close enough for me to stab him. Then how quickly I'd need to move to the other side of the room to lure the second man there.

In my mind, I envisioned the escape. I imagined every step of the way that would lead me toward the window, keys in my hand, enabled to get out of here and flee.

Tomorrow, it will be time.

Nodding to myself, I went through the routine again, faking the attack and danger that would come as I fought back and escaped. Like a mime stuck in a never-ending rehearsal, I prepared to fight my captors and get away.

Because if I couldn't, if I didn't, it wouldn't just be my life on the line.

My unborn baby's life depended on this escape.

My unwed sister's fate relied on my ability to flee and return to her at home.

I won't let anyone hurt you. I vowed it as I stared out the window, placing my hand over my stomach once more as though I could protect the precious new life that grew there just by covering the slight bump that was already growing from my one night with the sexy stranger.

I'd been hurt and tortured enough for one lifetime, and I'd be damned if I wouldn't do all that I could to prevent any more harm intended for my family.

4

BEN

Lev didn't reach out to me again about the hit on O'Malley. In the days after his wedding, that night his father-in-law fell over dead at the reception, he failed to resume contacting me about the hit the Baranovs wanted done.

I didn't expect him to follow up so soon. He was busy. With Eva as his new wife and this sudden death at the oddest timing, of course, he was busy.

But he wasn't the only one busy about Boris Baranov falling over dead. I wanted to know what happened that night, too. Actively investigating it was my course of action.

And that was why I was under disguise as a waiter at an Ilyin-owned restaurant uptown. It was a perfect and simple cover to listen in on Igor Petrov and Geoff Ilyin, one of the leaders for that family. Those two leaders had come here to discuss the very same matter that was on everyone's minds—Boris's death. It had rocked the Mafia world, and no one would claim the death or admit they'd acted on murder.

"You didn't have him killed that night?" Geoff asked Igor, his face stern and impatient.

"No." Igor scoffed, smirking. "Why would I waste time putting a hit on Boris Baranov? He was a useless drunk with no power."

Geoff nodded. "But you *have* wasted time putting other hits out before." His smile was taunting and cruel.

"Oh, shut up." Igor scowled, clearly displeased with this reminder.

"Only you would try to save money and hire amateurs to take out a Baranov," Geoff said wryly.

"Yes, to take out Oleg. Not Boris," Igor replied. "And it's not my fault I tried to shop around." He rubbed the back of his head, frowning as he seemed to think back to that time. "I couldn't get ahold of that one militant, Warner."

Liar.

Igor Petrov had contacted me and asked me to take out Oleg Baranov. I hadn't made up my mind on accepting that job, though. Too impatient for action, Igor had instead gone to subpar amateur killers for hire—who'd failed. All they'd done was put a bullet in Rurik's arm when he'd guarded his boss.

"We're still not pleased about how things shook out with the hit *we* put on Lev Kvashnin." Geoff lifted his chin and looked down at Igor. "The hit you agreed to assist us with."

I remained ramrod straight, posing like the other waiters in the room. We were expected to blend in and be at the ready like slaves or butlers, it seemed, but I worried that we'd be expected to exit the room with this conversation continuing. I hoped not. I had to assume after this bickering that these two men would talk more about who could've killed Boris.

Igor shook his head, narrowing his eyes as he lifted his hands in a truce. "No. No. You don't get to be mad at me. I told you before. I had nothing to do with Irina helping Lev escape your warehouse. I've disowned that bitch."

"She helps Lev escape," Geoff growled, "and then turns traitor to marry into the Baranov family. It looks awfully suspicious from my perspective."

"Don't remind me," Igor snapped. "That ungrateful bitch is nothing to me. Nothing. She doesn't represent the Petrov power."

Geoff didn't reply, still looking displeased but not pushing the matter any further.

"Did *you* try to have Boris killed at that reception?" Igor asked, as if he wanted to move past the topic of his daughter not siding with him.

It was Geoff's turn to show an annoyed expression. "No. Why would I? Like you said, Boris is a waste of space. No one will miss him."

"But do you think someone else could've had him killed?" Igor asked. "Another enemy who is trying to use him as a diversion?"

Geoff shrugged. "How would that work? No one would care whether Boris lived or died."

Igor didn't agree if his doubtful expression was any indication. "He's a waste. Even Oleg would agree with that. But he's still a Baranov, and killing any member of that family would be viewed as an attack."

I thought so too. It didn't matter if Boris didn't have much power in the organization. He was still a member. But I didn't suspect another outsider or other enemy of sending a message to Oleg with Boris's death.

I'd become something of an expert with these Mafia Families, taking and passing on hits from all of them in the New York circle of crime. No one could call the Baranovs their enemies like the Petrovs and Ilyins did. Their antagonism was obvious, sometimes irritatingly so, but both loathed Oleg's family above all else.

"Maybe so." Geoff shrugged. "But I haven't heard of any other organization scheming to bring down the Baranovs. Not even the Cartel, and they're building up near the ports again."

Igor slitted his eyes. His ruddy face reddened as he showed his fury. "But the Baranovs must be ended. I'll be damned if Oleg Baranov remains in power any longer."

Geoff nodded, sipping his coffee, as though he'd heard this like a broken record.

"I want the Baranovs killed. I want their power and reach reduced."

Geoff nodded some more, dismissing Igor with a wave. "I know. We want the same thing, but Igor, you are worrying about nothing."

Staying still, I tried my best not to look like I was soaking up all that was said. Incriminating plans were being shared here, and I was grateful to be this informed as an independent player.

"Worrying about nothing?" Igor spluttered. "How the fuck can you think this is *nothing*?"

"Because the Baranovs will be ended. Their power will be cut down to nothing." Geoff grinned slowly. "Eric Benson will see to it."

Igor furrowed his brow. "The politician? That young Benson kid?"

"He's not so young now," Geoff argued lightly. "He's all grown up, ready to go into office, following in his father's footsteps. And like his father, Eric will prove instrumental in removing the Baranov power. He'll side with us and make it impossible for the Baranovs to get away with anything anymore. He'll have his agencies come down hard on them all."

Damn. They never stop. It was no secret that the government was corrupt. Plenty of people in the courts and in the capital looked the other way when crime families were being charged. A little money deposited here or there, and things were taken care of.

"That's not going to do anything quickly," Igor said. "And that's never a guarantee. Benson might say he'll side with us, but until that happens, it's all talk."

Geoff shook his head. "Not this time. We've been playing the long game here, Igor. The Ilyins had the eldest Baranov daughter taken and held so she could be married off to Eric. Once a member of the Baranov family is part of the Benson family, they will have leverage and the ability to destroy the Baranovs from the inside out."

Yeah, right. Again, I resisted making a face at his claims. Sure, arranged marriages were commonplace in the Mafia, and they could be used as a way to control or manipulate other families. But this was Oleg, and he didn't bend to others. I had already noticed what a formidable man he could be.

"I'm not sure your supposed long game will pan out how you want it to. So you force a Baranov to be the politician's wife. That isn't a guarantee that this Benson guy would do anything we'd expect."

"He would," Geoff insisted. "And Eric Benson will also have the backing from O'Malley, the next governor to be sworn in." His smile was smug. "It will all be fine."

For you.

I followed the other waiters as they moved toward a coffee station. In this private room of the restaurant, intended for hosting secret meetings like these, the guests were served and pampered.

Moving on autopilot while I spied, I ruminated over all that was said. As an outsider looking—or listening—in, I could read between the lines.

According to what Geoff said, it seemed like this "long game" of having that daughter kidnapped to make her marry into the politician's family would benefit the Ilyins. *Only* the Ilyins, not the Petrovs too.

For not the first time, I wondered if these two Mafia outfits would cancel each other out. They were both too eager to eliminate the Baranovs, but they weren't actual allies with each other. That old saying about an enemy of one's enemy being a friend could hold true, but in this case, I couldn't believe that Igor and Geoff would actually be friends.

My hesitation seemed wise now. With how quick the Petrovs and Ilyins seemed to bicker and point fingers, it was smart not to be loyal with either of them. Both had been hiring me to do hits. Igor hired me to take out Yusef Ilyin, a drug dealer, but then Lev ended up killing him. Geoff and his family didn't know that Igor was the man behind Yusef's death, and if they did, I bet they'd put a hit out on Igor himself.

They're all morons. I could only guess how long the Petrov-Ilyin grudges and scrimmages would last, but the one thing that remained constant was how the Baranovs didn't fuck around with that nonsense.

Moments later, I filed out of the room with the waiters. I couldn't linger in that dining room as a solo worker to hear anything else the two men would say, but I had a hunch I'd gotten all that I could from them.

As I left, I considered all that I'd learned. Most importantly, their attitudes further convinced me that I would do better not to take any more work from them. They were both going down, as far as I could tell.

But how much more work should I even take? I'd been at this for a long time. Killing was a solid career, but I was tired.

I was formerly in the military after being rejected by my Mafia relatives in Russia. Going independent had served me well. But now, as the big four-oh loomed near, I considered the option of not doing this alone anymore. Turning forty wasn't a real milestone. My age was just a number, but somehow, it had been getting to me.

If I had to be honest about it, I'd admit that I wouldn't mind settling and slowing down. I wouldn't suffer from having a crew or team again, too. Backup would be nice if I wanted to finally make time for a wife and family.

Family? Now that I was away from the building and leaving the area, I felt free to huff out loud and roll my eyes. I was being ridiculous, thinking about settling down that much. Everyone was prone to midlife-crisis thoughts at some stage of their lives, but this was crazy talk.

A wife? A family?

I shook my head and stuffed my hands in my pockets. Neither of those fanciful things would make sense, not for me. No woman ever stayed on my mind for long—not like that sexy brunette upstate had.

I had yet to forget about her, but the more I thought back to how eager she was to lose her virginity to a stranger, insisting we didn't share anything past our first names—which she could've lied about—I knew she wasn't wife material. Sonya, as she'd claimed for her alias, had only been looking for a good time.

And it had been a good time. Showing her how to take what I gave her had been one of the sexiest experiences of my life. I'd never met a more responsive woman. Just thinking about her had me smiling and starting to get turned on.

But I'd never see her again. We'd made sure of that by keeping ourselves as strangers together for the night.

"Besides, I've got no time for that," I mumbled to myself.

A woman? A family? Slowing down?

Nah. Not now.

Right now, I had to decide about the current jobs I'd been approached about, like O'Malley. Even Oleg Baranov.

Keeping my finger on the pulse of this antagonism between the Petrovs and Ilyins would require my attention too.

No time for a woman now.

It *was* time to get ahold of Lev, though. I had to make up my mind about whether I wanted to work with the Baranovs at all.

5

SONYA

Icy rain dripped down from the branches overhead. No leaves blocked the light precipitation out here in this dense wood line. Every chilling drop landed on my matted down hair until it collected at the back of my neck and slithered along my spine.

Shivers racked my body, but I didn't pay any further notice to the cold. Or how wet I was.

Clutching the bloody butter knife in my hand, I scanned the lone building ahead of me.

I wasn't sure I'd ever let go of the measly little dull blade I'd used to secure my freedom. It had seemed like a miracle when the guards hadn't noticed the butter knife missing from my food tray. My meek demeanor had served me well for so long. The more docile and beaten-down I'd seemed, the looser they'd gotten with watching my every move.

The first time I suspected I could be pregnant—when my period was late and I felt so crampy—I started making the plans to escape. Tucking that butter knife under the edge of my mattress was the first step. Ramming it into the guard's neck yesterday was another step.

The dull blade hadn't made my first murder very clean or easy, but I'd done it. I ended his life when he came in to transport me to this Benson man for marriage. Then when the Ilyin guard's partner lunged at me to constrain me, I fought him with every fiber of my being, every ounce of hatred.

Hours had passed. The night had fallen and receded. Time still carried on in a blur, though, and I hoped this shell-shocked fugue would lift.

I did it.

I'm out.

I'm free.

But as I hunkered down in the trees out here, spying on this lonely little house in what seemed like the middle of nowhere, I wasn't homebound just yet.

I had no phone. No money. No clothes except the bloody, torn ones I wore now. Slippers covered my freezing, raw feet. While I had no idea how far I was from New York, how distant I was from the Baranov mansion I longed to return to, I was well aware that I had a journey to survive.

Getting out of captivity was the initial phase of reclaiming my life.

But ensuring I was back to safety and out of the Ilyins' reach was another challenge.

I blinked, preventing more of the cool spring drizzle from dripping into my eyes. Moving my eyelids was all the motion I wanted to allow as I tensed and debated.

No one had gone into that house. No one had exited either. And I'd know. I had been watching the building since the darkest hour of the night. Now in the morning, as the sun rose through the gray sky, I waited some more to guess whether this place would be safe.

Banking on the goodwill of strangers felt so risky, but I wasn't naïve to think I could get home like this, on my own.

Forcing down a swallow, I ignored the hunger pangs that wouldn't quit. My mouth and throat were so dry and raw, too. Water would be a blessing. Food would help too. But no matter how long I sat and crouched out here like a wild animal on the run, I wouldn't know if the residents in that small house would lend me a hand until I asked.

Just get closer. See if anyone's there.

I stood, wincing at the pain of staying low for so long. The wet cold wasn't ideal, but I couldn't bring myself to care. I was here. I was alive and able to choose my own path for the first time in over a decade. Mafia princesses were expected to be pampered and spoiled, but those had both been beaten out of me years ago. I would set the bar low.

Leaves crunched underfoot as I gingerly advanced toward the house. My stomach remained tied in knots, but every difficult swallow I managed pushed that nausea back.

Someone's in there. The lights shining from behind the curtains was proof. Tantalizing and addicting, the scent of a meaty stew cooking inside suggested someone was making a meal.

Growls erupted from my stomach, but I ignored them, determined to reach the door.

Please, please don't be scared.

Please care enough to help me.

Please.

I looked a fright, muddy, bloody, and worn ragged. But I didn't pose a threat. I couldn't, not when I was so weak and desperate for help.

Shit.

The knife.

This thin scrap of metal was supposed to be used for spreading butter, but with the blood coated on it, I *would* look deranged and deadly. Trembling with the energy needed to move, I lowered my arm to drop the butter knife. I couldn't knock on a door and beg for help when I held a weapon, but my panic rose with giving up my only means of defense.

Thumping onto the welcome mat at the door, the knife settled on the surface. Within seconds, the rain pattered down on it and began to rinse it clean.

I raised my hand to knock on the door. Even that pressure stung my cold knuckles, sore from fighting the Ilyin guard yesterday morning. Before I lost the willpower to stand much longer, I nudged the butter knife aside until it scooted off the mat. It slid, falling into the mulch and leaves beneath a bush.

Footsteps sounded inside. Light and quick, they approached the door.

Please be a woman. Please be a kind, sweet, generous stranger of a woman.

As if I'd jinxed it, louder, heavier footsteps joined in.

Dammit.

It would be just my luck that the first house I'd stumble upon would have a man inside it.

Too late.

I blinked, forcing my sluggish lids to remain open. Nausea returned. Fatigue swept over me. I raised my hand again to knock, having to take my chances that someone who lived here would help me. But I didn't complete the action. Slanting toward the closed door, I heaved out a deep exhale and kept my fist on the wood. Leaning forward more and more, I let my eyes close as I focused on the bare minimum of breathing.

I was tired. Thirsty. Hungry. Nauseated and exhausted.

But I was *free*.

As the door was pulled open, I lacked the energy to open my eyes. I was free—free falling. Heat wafted out from the interior of the house, and with the bone-deep need for comfort as I hit the last reserves of my energy, I pitched forward and passed out, hopefully into the residence of good Samaritans who would care to keep me alive.

Later, when I woke from the deep darkness of a solid slumber, I instinctively knew that I was still free. The scent of delicious stew accompanied a cozy warmth. Soft pillows and the satiny smoothness of sheets and blankets soothed my raw skin.

I wasn't on that property anymore. I wasn't back at that house where my mother was raped and killed, where Ilyin men held me captive so they'd dictate a future I didn't want.

Instead, I slowly opened my eyes to the interior of a small bedroom. A redheaded woman furrowed her brow as she peered down at me. Freckles dotted her cheeks and nose, making her seem youthful and juvenile, but as she realized I was waking, a maternal sense of concern covered her face.

"Kyle, she's waking up," she said calmly to someone else in the house.

Fuck. A man. She's not alone.

She backed up from her seat next to the bed I lay on. As she lifted her hand, a wedding ring sparkled in the low light. "Easy," she urged gently. "You're okay. You'll be all right."

A man huffed a low chuckle as he came into view. A tall, burly man smiled at me as he carried a baby. "She's a woman, Jenny. Not one of the stray dogs you see at the clinic."

Jenny smiled more, glancing at the man as he rocked the baby in his arms. "I am aware of that, Mister."

"She's a vet, not a doctor," Kyle said teasingly as he glanced at me watching them both so cautiously. "But as my wife likes to remind me when stray animals come to the door, all mammals can benefit from the same basics of first aid."

"And people are mammals, too," Jenny quipped at her husband as she extended a straw toward me. "Water?"

I sipped the icy drink, going too quickly and ending up coughing.

"Easy," she urged again. "You're safe here."

But am I?

I doubted I'd feel safe until I got home and saw my sister, all who would be left of the family I once had.

"Take it slow," Kyle said, nodding as he continued rocking with the baby. "I'm Kyle Peterson, and this is my wife Jenny," he introduced. "Do you know your name?"

Finished with the water, I debated what to tell them. I couldn't risk their knowing I was a Mafia princess on the loose. After I killed and beat off the guards at the house, I took the keys from them and sped away in the van that was likely intended for my transport. A vehicle was a faster way to leave, but it had also ensured other guards would chase after me.

I hadn't driven anything before, and my reckless race from that property had ended up with a crash. Afterward, I'd run as far and fast as I could and I now had no clue where I was. I was ignorant of my location. I wanted to know if I'd gotten far enough from the Ilyins' property to be confident that these strangers wouldn't report my presence here.

"It's okay," Jenny said, clearly guessing I struggled with amnesia. "You can trust us." Perhaps she was wisely guessing I struggled more with trusting anyone. "You can lie low. Recover. Relax. We will keep you safe here."

Tears stung at my lids, and I gave up the fight to hold them back.

"Oh, it's okay," she said softly, offering me tissues. "It will be okay."

I'd yearned to hear someone tell me that. I wished to have someone—anyone—convince me that there was a way out of misery. Jenny and Kyle had no clue how far from *okay* I was, but I would forever treasure their being good, decent people to give a shit about a strange woman down on her luck.

Over the next few days, that was all they did. They cared. They gave me a warm bed to sleep in, food to eat, water to drink. Not once did they push for answers, giving me space and time to accept that I was safe. Eventually, though, once they showed that I would be safe here, Jenny grew bolder to ask me more questions.

"Do you know how far along you are?" she asked when she handed me clean clothes after a shower.

I shook my head.

Jenny frowned and nodded as she backed up and closed the bathroom door, intuiting that I wanted privacy.

"Were you—"

"I wasn't raped," I answered, guessing where she was leading with this. "I was taken by..." I couldn't identify the Ilyins. She could alert them. "I was taken by some men and—"

"It's okay," Jenny replied from the other side of the door. "I... You don't need to relive it or talk or anything like that. Take your time. Kyle was just worried and he's been wondering if we should call the cops or—"

I lunged over to open the door quickly. "No. Please, no."

The cops weren't allies of mine. I was a Mafia princess. No Mafia family wanted to rely on the same law and order normal people like Jenny and Kyle would. We had our own law and order, our own justice system. But she couldn't understand that.

Jenny held her hands up in a truce. "Okay. Cool. I get it."

I narrowed my eyes. "You do?"

She nodded, calm. "I do. My dad was an alcoholic."

I couldn't help a scoff. "Mine too."

Still, she remained chill and unbothered as she led me back to the tiny guest room so I could lie down. Just walking to the bathroom tired me so much.

"My father was an abusive alcoholic and the cops, the social workers, all of them" —she rolled her eyes— "none of them would actually help. So, yeah. I get it."

"Do you need a hand?" Kyle asked as Jenny guided me back to the room. He sat with the infant, rocking in a chair.

"No. We're okay," Jenny replied. She seemed to respect that I was more at ease with her, not her husband, but it was sort of silly. Kyle was clearly a gentle giant, a stay-at-home dad with their young baby son they'd named Damon. He couldn't be a danger to me. Still, I was wary of another man nearby.

In my room again, Jenny helped me lower to the bed. She'd already checked me over. Even though she was a vet and worked with animals, she was medically knowledgeable. She tended to my cuts and bruises. She checked my lungs and heart. She even checked on the baby, the best that she could without an ultrasound machine or anything high-tech at home.

Over the past couple of days, she'd explained who she was and where I found them. Maybe she thought opening up about herself would put me at ease while I struggled to speak up about who I was. Perhaps she still feared I had amnesia or something.

I didn't. I couldn't trust her with *my* story, though, so I appreciated her filling the silence with her gentle voice. She was a vet at a clinic in town, and Kyle was home with her on paternity leave since she'd just given birth to their baby boy a month ago. While she didn't mention anything about a woman being missing or anything that might have to do with the Ilyins, I couldn't take faith that I was far enough away. She did explain that they lived in a small town in New York, though, and she had commented that the city was three hours away.

Staying quiet about who I was and what I needed to do was the safest option. I knew that the second I said I was a member of a Mafia family, they could cast me out and not want anything to do with criminals. I suspected that the moment I gave them permission to contact the cops about a wounded stray woman showing up, the Ilyins could track me somehow.

But I couldn't stay. I couldn't put them at risk for helping me, and I wouldn't give up on my mission to get home to Eva. After their kindness, offering me help without expecting a single thing in return, I was resolved to leave before they could be in danger for assisting me. There was simply no way for me to know how far or near the Ilyins could be, and I refused to put this small family in harm's way.

As I lay in bed, hearing Kyle and Jenny in the kitchen as they made dinner, cared for the baby, and acted like an innocent, sweet trio, I fought the tears and wished I could have that. I envied their peaceful home and lives out here in the woods.

From the bottom of my heart, I wished that I could be a contented mother to this baby in my belly, comfortable and safe. That my child's father could be there with me, present and helping, not a distant memory of a one-night stand. That we'd have a home, a *real* family.

Dreams could be sweet like that, but as I relaxed this one last night and accepted their generosity before I could leave, I guarded myself from letting these wistful visions cloud my brain too much.

I could fantasize all I wanted, but I had to remain level-headed and focused.

I'd escaped.

And now it was time to survive and return to the city for the security I could receive there.

Come dawn, while they slept in, I'd sneak out and figure out how to get *home*. I had been gone too damn long, and I had to ensure a new future of my own choosing.

6

BEN

After hearing Igor and Geoff talking about the Baranovs and their mutual desire to bring the family down, I felt more inclined to accept that hit Lev wanted done. I wasn't ready to sign up as an official ally of the Baranovs, but I was more intrigued about what it could be like if I leaned on them and affiliated exclusively with them.

Unfortunately, Lev wasn't easily accessible. He'd gone through the proper channels to reach out to me. He'd left messages on my encrypted lines to give me the heads up that he was interested in my services. I still wanted more details before making my decision, and that was a caution I harbored before accepting any job. In order to discuss this hit on O'Malley further, I'd need to locate Lev and pin him down long enough to hold a conversation. Since Boris's death, though, he was nearly unreachable.

I soon found out why. Oleg Baranov was in the hospital, and as the boss's apparent right-hand man, Lev was there often.

Eva was the one who'd let that secret out. When trying to hack into the mansion's main phone lines, I picked up on her call to Irina. It seemed that Oleg had suffered a health scare, some kind of a cardiac event, and he was being supervised at the nearest hospital. Word hadn't traveled about Oleg's health, though. The Baranovs were cautious for anyone to get word that the big leader was declining.

I doubted Oleg *was* declining. Now that I'd adopted a disguise as a health aide to sneak into Oleg's private suite at the hospital, I saw the evidence of him very much alive, if sedated and asleep. If anyone wanted my unofficial opinion, Oleg could do well with cutting out some of those cigars, but he didn't seem to be on death's door. The nurses and doctors there had the same thoughts. Even though I'd snuck in here to confront Lev and talk to him about that job, I wouldn't dismiss the intel I was gathering about Oleg's condition while I was at it.

"He is stable," one doctor told Lev again.

"Then why isn't he awake?" the Baranov soldier said. He rubbed his hand over his jaw, antsy as he peered at Oleg sleeping in the bed.

"His heart needs to recover. Rest is important and—"

"But you're not sedating him as heavily anymore, right?" Vik asked. He was here with Lev, visiting—or overseeing—Oleg's care.

"Correct." The doctor nodded as a nurse filed out of the room.

I busied myself with pretending to tidy and organize the medical supplies on the cart near Oleg's bed. Tubes ran from him and plenty of patches were left as stickers on his skin. The Baranov leader was unconscious and still, but his vitals seemed normal on the panel connected to him.

"He is receiving a lower dose of sedation, and as his recovery continues, we will adjust our plans accordingly." With one more nod, this one as an acknowledgement or farewell, the man turned to leave.

Without any other medical staff in the room except for me, the two soldiers studied their leader.

"You think this has to do with Boris's death?" Vik asked.

Lev shook his head. "No. We've ruled out any foul play. Boris died because he was an overweight alcoholic. The autopsy proved it." He glanced at Vik. "Boris wasn't killed. He just died—no surprise about that. Therefore, it's ridiculous to worry that someone tried to kill Oleg."

Vik scoffed. "Ridiculous? Don't tell Rurik that. He took a bullet from the last time someone tried to kill Oleg."

"Yeah, yeah." Lev shoved his hands in his pockets. "Someone will always be out to get him. Or us. But I don't think Boris's death caused Oleg to have a heart attack."

Heart attack, huh? I didn't intend to share this news with anyone, but I felt better to have all the facts possible.

"What about the stress, though?" Vik asked as he crossed his arms then sighed. "If the stress about Boris dying could've caused Oleg to have that heart attack."

"Maybe if Oleg was fond of his brother."

"Which we know he wasn't." Vik smirked. "Oleg tolerated Boris."

"We all did," Lev said wryly.

"Then I fear the stress about his search for Sonya is taking a toll on him," Vik replied.

Sonya?

At the mention of *that* name, I furrowed my brow and dropped a packet of tissues that I was putting away on the cart.

That was *her* name. Sonya was the name, or alias, of my gorgeous virgin who'd been game for a one-night stand with me upstate. I'd been in the area to kill an Ilyin soldier, a simple little hit to pass the time. Sonya had been a pleasant surprise on a boring night in that small town, but it was strange that I still couldn't shake her from my mind. She was imprinted on me somehow, but I figured it was just because I knew I'd never see her again.

Plenty of women could be named Sonya.

But which Sonya was Oleg searching for?

What is he talking about?

Realizing Lev hadn't commented on Vik's remark yet, I lifted my gaze to watch the two Baranov men in the reflection of the glass door to the cabinet on the wall. As I did, I locked into direct eye contact with Lev.

He narrowed his eyes, watching me through the reflection. His lips flattened as he stepped forward, and I reacted. Spinning quickly, I had just enough time to deflect his grab at my arm. Vik was no slouch, though. He had to have noticed Lev's attention on me, and with my immediate move to defend myself, he snapped to focus.

"You!" Lev scowled. "I thought you looked familiar."

"Me?" I feigned innocence, smoothing down the hospital uniform I'd borrowed for this cover. "I'm just—"

"Just the fucker who's been everywhere and nowhere at all." His gaze sharpened as he snarled. Vik remained alert and tense at his side, as if waiting to jump in and hold him back. Or attack me with him.

I raised my brows in a silent question, goading him on to explain.

"Ben fucking Warner, huh?" Lev guessed, pointing at my face. "I remember when I killed you at Yusef Ilyin's cabin."

I smiled slowly, shaking my head. "That was supposed to be *my* hit, by the way."

"It was?" Lev asked, not lightening up yet.

"Someone else had a hit on him?" Vik asked. "Who?"

I glanced at him. "You've been catching up since coming out of the whorehouse, huh?" I teased of him.

Vik scoffed but refrained from glaring at me like Lev was. I expected this conversation to be confrontational, but at least one of them wasn't a hothead.

"What *don't* you know about us?" Vik muttered.

"I do my research." I made it my business to know the Mafia's business, including how Vik had gone from supervising a whorehouse to being something more of an upper leader within the organization. "Yet I still don't know enough details about why you've contacted me to kill O'Malley." There was no point reclaiming my cover. I came here to talk to Lev, and now that I had his attention, my disguise was no longer necessary. It was time to cut the crap.

"What the fuck?" Lev sneered at me. "I reached out to you weeks ago, and you've been impossible to get ahold of since."

I shrugged. "I tend to stay mobile."

"And now you sneak in here to spy on *us*?" He pointed at himself.

I had to tread carefully now. Given how secretive they were being about Oleg's condition, I couldn't be cocky about getting in and up close without their knowing. Sneaking around and being stealthy was all part of the thrill. Killing my hits was the ultimate high, but I loved doing this clandestine shit. It fed the sick and twisted part of my soul, knowing I could always trick and fool others so easily.

"I came here for a chance to talk to you about this hit you wanted to hire me for."

"You snuck in here like this to accomplish that?" he accused.

"Well, I've got your attention now. We can talk." When he didn't lose the scowl, I added, "You've been a hard man to get ahold of lately."

"Ever hear of a fucking phone?" he shot back.

"I prefer obtaining my information in person."

"And undercover?" Vik arched a brow.

"What the hell do you need more information for?" Lev glanced at Oleg and frowned. "I reached out with a job for you to kill O'Malley. I gave you a price. If it's not enough, we can negotiate."

Wow. That was impressive. Hiring a contract killer wasn't cheap. The price wasn't my issue, but the fact that the Baranovs could spend accordingly made them stand out even more. These guys were so… normal, not cheapskates like Petrovs or the Ilyins.

"What more do you need to know?" Lev demanded.

"For starters, why you wanted him dead," I said.

Lev laughed. It was a single, rough bark of a sound as he tossed his head back. "Give me a goddamn break, you asshole. You want to know *why*? What the hell does it matter? It's a hit. It's a job. Are you growing a conscience or something now?"

"I prefer to be informed of all the consequences that could follow my potential kills."

"Potential." Lev smirked, seeming amused instead of just pissed off that I'd been eavesdropping here. Or maybe he was more irritated with the fact that I delayed accepting a job from him, that I liked to do things my way, not his. "A potential kill. You make it sound like you're unsure you can handle a hit job. Then again, if someone hired you to kill Yusef but I beat you to it, maybe you're not the elite assassin everyone's making you out to be, after all."

Oh, fuck you. My patience would wane really fast if he was going to be a cocky asshole.

"Who hired you to kill Yusef?" Lev asked.

It wasn't my nature to share details. I was the one who asked the questions and got answers. Something about this fucker intrigued me, though. Lev was hotheaded, but he didn't seem to be a petty moron like other Mafia men I dealt with. "Igor Petrov."

Lev rolled his eyes. "That's hilarious," he said, deadpan.

"Wait. So Yusef Ilyin fucked us over with that drug deal…" Vik said.

"Which pissed *him* off to the point that he'd ask me to kill Yusef," Lev finished for him, gesturing at Oleg on the bed.

"Then Igor hired you"—Vik addressed me—"to kill Yusef…"

"And then later, he'd help the Ilyins capture me in retaliation for my killing Yusef," Lev said, completing Vik's observation.

I shrugged. "Sounds about right."

"Fucking Petrov," Lev and Vik said in unison.

"If it's any consolation, I'm confident you're not the only one with that sentiment." Igor had quite the reputation for stirring up shit and trying to come out on top.

"But I killed you," Lev said, narrowing his eyes. "The day I finally got to Yusef, you were 'guarding' him and I shot you."

"Nothing a face mask can't fix. I had a body double end up as that carcass." I grinned.

Lev studied me for a long moment. "So, what is it? You're some kind of ex-military spy? Master of disguise and pain in the ass who had a conscience about whom he kills now?"

"Sort of. You can form your own opinions of me." Now that I had him talking, I wondered how I could get them back to the person I really wanted to know more about.

Sonya.

There was no way that they could be talking about my one-night stand. There was also no guarantee that Sonya was her real name.

Something nagged at me, though. Now that I'd heard "her" name, and I kept dreaming about her every time I fell asleep…

"What were you talking about earlier? About Oleg being so stressed out about looking for Sonya."

Lev huffed a laugh. "Who the fuck do you think you are? It's none of your business what we were talking about. Your only business with the Baranov family is whether or not you want us to hire you to kill O'Malley."

He was right. So far, that was the only connection between us. But I couldn't give up on this mention of Sonya.

"Who's Sonya?" I asked again, as if he hadn't shot my line of questioning down.

"None of your business," Lev repeated.

"Why do you want to know?" Vik asked.

Dammit. They weren't going to tell me shit. They were too guarded, and rightly so. If I had to guess, this Sonya woman was a member of their family, and that, again, impressed me. Lev and Vik stood in for Oleg, and with their attitudes, it was clear that they were decent enough to be protective of their women. It cut such a contrast to how Igor and Geoff had spoken about the women in this world—nothing more than disgraces or pawns in their eyes.

It was time for me to cooperate if I wanted more intel about anything else.

"You know what? I'll do it. I'll accept the hit on O'Malley." This way, actively working for them would give me more chances for me to overhear anything else they might say about Sonya.

Come on. There's no fucking way it's her, right?

Lev accepted my offered hand and shook it, but he eyed me cautiously. "This stays between us."

"All my jobs are confidential."

Lev nodded. "Good. Then maybe after you finish the hit on O'Malley, we could hire you for this one." He glanced at his sleeping leader. "We all assumed they were killed years ago, but just in case, it wouldn't hurt to have extra help. So he doesn't have to stress about it anymore."

Vik nodded. "It'd be nice to have answers once and for all. And he wouldn't stress over it ever again."

"Stress about what?" I asked, volleying my gaze between the two men.

"About finding Sonya, his niece who went missing eleven years ago." Lev watched me closely.

What? "Oleg's *niece?*" I asked as my heart beat faster.

"Yeah," Vik said. "Eva's older sister."

Oh, fuck.

Lev narrowed his eyes, still watching me so intensely. I was damned good at masking my emotions, but the reason for my nagging feeling was revealed fully now. Lev was right to notice and be suspicious of the shocked expression I tried and failed to hide. Because it hit me like a punch in the gut.

Sonya.

It wasn't just the mention of my one-night stand's name that had her on my mind. Since the moment I saw Eva at the mansion, I'd struggled with how similar the women were. That was what nagged me.

And now, I knew why—because they bore a resemblance to each other as *sisters*!

I hadn't taken a sexy stranger's virginity at that shitty bar upstate over three months ago.

I'd claimed a lost Mafia princess's virginity.

Sonya Baranov was my one-night stand.

"So the sooner you do this hit for us…" Lev said evenly, jarring me out of my reverie.

I nodded, taking a step back and holding up my hand to cut him off. "Right. I heard you." The news that I'd slept with a Mafia princess blew my mind. "Kill O'Malley. Then track down…"

"Sonya," Lev said.

"It—" I cleared my throat, furrowing my brow as I let this news sink into my brain. "Uh, it'd be my pleasure."

I didn't need him to order me to find her.

I'd already been struggling with missing her, anyway.

7

SONYA

Just before dawn, I stared at the paper and hesitated at the sound.

Baby Damon stirred and made a noise from the bassinet, but Jenny and Kyle didn't get up. Nonetheless, I waited another moment for the house to be quiet again.

Okay. All good.

Nothing was *good* about this. I felt terrible to pocket the four hundred dollars that I found stashed in this little lock box in a cabinet in the kitchen. I'd snooped for cash lying around and this was a decent start. The Petersons would have to make do without a truck I'd spotted out the window, too. Robbing these generous innocents wasn't something I wanted to do, but I had to get out of here.

I'd run away before an Ilyin could track me here and hurt them for assisting me.

I'd flee before any other obstacles could stop me from getting home to Eva.

But first, I had to appease my conscience. Putting the tip of the pen to the paper, I sighed and wrote a simple promise.

Thank you for your help. I will not forget how selfless you've been with me when you found me at my lowest.

IOU

-S

It seemed like such a paltry message for the couple who'd saved me. I passed out hoping they'd take me in for a night, and they had, without expecting anything in return. Food, water, warmth, comfort. Jenny was a saint to have given me those things. Kyle, too, had given me the dream of having a husband and family for my own baby. Mr. and Mrs. Peterson would wake up mad that I'd taken their things, but as soon as I was home, they would be rewarded richly.

First, I took the slim bag I'd packed with Jenny's things. A couple of changes of clothes that I hoped she wouldn't miss, some protein bars and apples, water bottles, the cash, and the keys. Outside, I put the rusty truck into neutral and began to push it down the drive. Once I was further from the house, I started the engine and sped off.

Without a driver's license, without any training of how to drive, I maneuvered the truck the best I could. I wasn't stupid. I'd witnessed men driving before, and it wasn't that hard once I got familiar with the feel of the engine.

Hours passed as I drove away, relying on a battered map I picked up at a diner. Everyone had phones, but I didn't. If I did, I doubted I'd know how to use them well. Technology sure had changed since I was kidnapped, but for the most part, the world outside that Ilyin property was the same as the one I'd been snatched from.

Jenny had asked me the first morning if there was anyone I'd wanted to call. Of course, there was. I wanted to speak with Eva. I wanted to contact the top guard and mightiest soldier of the Baranov organization. Maybe that one orphan, Lev, was still working for the family.

Uncle Oleg had just found him a few years before I was taken. If he was around at home, he'd be a good guard. My cousins, too. Rurik came to mind. So did Vik and several others.

Yet, I declined Jenny's offer. I knew none of their numbers. I didn't want to risk a call being traceable to the Petersons.

They had to already be suspicious when I said I didn't want the cops contacted.

But as I drove south, toward the city, I wished I did have a means of communication. I wanted a way to get news too. The TV monitors at gas stations and diners looked so high-tech and new, nothing like the TVs I recalled before I was kidnapped. On one hand, I marveled at how many things had evolved since I was taken. On the other hand, I was pissed that the fucking Ilyins had kept me so damn sheltered. Still, if I were to ask anyone for news about the Baranov family in New York City, it would out me as a member of the Mafia, and I damn well knew better than to make that mistake.

I drove Kyle's truck as far as I could. Well into the day, I burned rubber off the tires, hoping that the couple wouldn't have called the cops on me for taking the truck. The license plate could be tracked. But that ended up not mattering. Halfway to the city, by my rough estimates, the engine started making a noise and stopped, coming to a whining stop on the side of a country road. I winced and knew I couldn't push this old thing any further.

No wonder it was just sitting out there and rusting.

Without a vehicle, I had to resort to hitchhiking. It seemed that there was some new thing called Uber that people used. A gas station attendant offered to call me one, but I wasn't sure how safe that could be. Going on the internet to arrange a ride with a stranger? How the hell was that supposed to be smart?

Hitchhiking didn't prove to be any better.

"Want a ride?"

That was the question I warded off in a small town I walked to. Every creepy asshole who asked me that got a no—or I pretended I didn't hear them. I'd killed that Ilyin guard with a butter knife, and I'd repeat that crime if I had to, this time with the steak knife I'd taken from the Petersons' kitchen.

Riding with a middle-aged woman turned out to be a mistake too. She was a druggie who damn near wrecked her car trying to force me into giving her all my cash. In terms of defense, my steak knife wasn't on a level playing field with her gun. But I was a Mafia princess. I was no weakling to death or gore. She didn't know who she was messing with, and my dormant memories of self-defense lessons from guards aided me in getting out of her car.

When I was stuck walking along the highway again, doing my best to ignore an ache in my heel from running away from that druggie who'd seemed helpful, I obsessed about what to do.

I'd escaped. I left the security of my rescuers in the woods. Now that I was on my way back to Eva, I looked even further ahead. By foot or in someone's car, I *would* get home. I would make my way to Eva, but I worried it could be too late.

Uncle Oleg was gone. So was my mother, and now, according to those Ilyin guards, my father. The whole Baranov family was coming apart, and I just couldn't let my sister be taken. She'd be vulnerable now without anyone else supporting her, but as soon as I was there, I'd make sure she wouldn't be sold to some unscrupulous fiancé.

But that's not enough.

Each time I took a painful step, walking through the downpour of rain that started, my anger and fury burned hotter and hotter.

I was taken once. Eva could be taken now. And still, the threat of being married off to this Benson man would loom large.

If the Ilyins dared to kidnap me and hold me captive for over a decade, they wouldn't give up easily.

Whatever they'd benefit from making this marriage happen could still be an option. They'd be more motivated to get me again and force me to marry that man, whoever he was. It was always about power. Always some unending game and war of leverage and strength.

However...

I narrowed my eyes as I trudged through the crappy spring storm.

"If I kill him…"

Then that won't be a possibility.

That seemed smartest. Having this Benson man killed and eliminated would be the surest way to avoid being his wife. It would remove the significance and motivation to kidnap me. While there was still so much more to learn, things I'd demand to know once I got home, I was certain that this plan would thwart them all and keep me and my sister safe.

And you. I lowered my hand to my stomach, proud that I'd gotten my unborn baby out of captivity. It was a miracle that he or she had been created. I'd always wanted a child, one of hopefully several. Before I was kidnapped and during my captivity, that maternal dream hadn't faded, but I never could've guessed I'd be a mother like this.

Nor could I have anticipated how protective I'd be. They weren't joking when they said the mama bear phenomenon hit.

"I'll get us home," I promised my baby.

"And I'll kill that man." I nodded, letting my anger fuel me to keep moving.

"One day, I'll find you a daddy, but it will be a man I choose, little one." My whispered promises wouldn't be broken, but as I muttered the vows, I wished I didn't have to choose a man. I wished that Ben, the sexy stranger who'd taken my virginity, could be with me again.

I couldn't explain it, how deeply he'd impacted me, but he had. Yes, he was my first, and I supposed everyone remembered their first. It was something deeper, though, something profound that made me miss my one-time lover from that bar. But it was stupid to get my hopes up that high and fantasize about seeing him again.

The next day, after sleeping in the woods under an old hunting stand, I walked the rest of the way into the city. As more sights became familiar, I registered how details had changed in some places and how other landmarks remained exactly the same.

Rain stopped falling, and I could move faster. Ubers seemed to be another version of taxi, which were paid for through an app. I didn't have a phone to pull that off, but I was glad an "old" taxi was waiting nearby as soon as I got into the city.

When I asked to be driven to the Baranov mansion, the driver laughed and kicked me out of the car.

"I ain't stupid," he growled. "That's where the Mafia live."

"No, it's not—"

He braked suddenly and got out of the driver's seat to open the back-door. "Out!"

For fuck's sake.

He sped off as soon as I got out of the car, but I realized not all hope was lost. He'd stopped on the block of one of Eva's favorite restaurants. Ever since she was a child, she'd loved this Italian place, and I prayed she might be near it today since it was evening time.

It felt like a long shot, but even if Eva wasn't here, a place she used to request going to weekly for their house salad dressing that she swore no other chef could make the same, I would be able to contact someone at home. I was sure of it. They'd know and respect the Baranov name. I bet I could ask the manager to just make a call and that would be it.

Inside the glitzy foyer of the restaurant, though, I spotted her.

She was here.

Eva. My sweet baby sister, all grown up. Tears gathered at my eyes as I stared at her across the room. After all these years, I would finally be reunited. I'd be back with my family! At last!

Taller and slimmer, she was so pretty and healthy looking. No longer the little girl I recalled, she was a mature, lovely woman, apparently dining with a couple of other women at her table.

I watched her stand. Mesmerized and partly fearing my eyes were playing tricks on me, I tracked her movements as she backed away from the table. She turned, heading toward the side as though she wanted to leave.

"No. Wait." I hurried forward, eager to catch her. "Eva!"

The hostess intervened immediately, stopping me from entering the dining room. "Excuse me."

"Let me go!"

Her arm barricaded me from entering. Another employee came to her assistance in blocking me. "This is for guests only."

"I'm—" I furrowed my brow, watching Eva head down the hallway, oblivious to the commotion I was causing at the entrance, too far away. "Eva! Wait! That's my sister. That's my—" I fought, shoving the restaurant employees back. Resisting their hold, I let my determination control me. "Let me go! I'm Sonya Bar— Let me *go*!"

More guests from the dining room turned, aware of my shouts as more security came closer. But I didn't stop fighting to get free.

Especially not when the two women at Eva's table turned to face me.

I gasped, stunned that a Petrov would be with her. "No!" Fighting harder, I broke away from the man and woman holding me back. They wouldn't be stronger than this need to protect Eva. Full of rage that the enemy would be near my baby sister, I raced forward. I recalled that girl from all those years ago. She was a Petrov, no doubt about it. Her name didn't matter. All Petrovs were enemies of the Baranovs. That couldn't have changed since I was in captivity. That wouldn't change in a million years.

"Eva!" I shouted it again as I ran toward the table. My sister had already walked away. But the Petrov stared at me defiantly, seated there like she had a right to be there. "You Petrov bitch. Stay away from her!"

Where are the guards? Why are they letting this Petrov near her?

"Hey. Stop!" Another woman, a short blonde at the table, stood and tried to step between me and the Petrov woman. "Get back."

"Don't you tell me to get back. I want her away from my sister!"

The blonde frowned. "What— Who—" She shook her head, confused yet still alarmed. "Your sister..."

"Where are the guards? Why is this woman near my sister?" I pointed at the Petrov seated at the table, then frantically scanned the room for Baranov guards who should come running. I didn't know who this blonde was. Or why Eva would be eating with a Petrov. Maybe they'd taken her? Maybe—

More restaurant employees rushed forward, eager to get me and drag me out of here. I'd caused a ruckus, disrupting the others eating here so much that the music couldn't be heard over the hostess and security guards shouting at me.

"Wait—" The blonde tried to grab my arm as I backed up.

More security guards came near, and I saw no sign of my sister, no sign of any of my family's guards. *What is going on?*

"Are you Sonya?" the blonde asked, incredulous.

Fuck. She knew me. Or she knew of me. This wasn't good. I couldn't risk anyone else recognizing me yet. Not until I reached Eva. Not until I saw my family first and understood what had been happening since I had been taken.

It was foolhardy to come out of hiding like this, without backup or support. How dumb was I to think I could just walk out of that Ilyin property and emerge into the society of the Mafia again?

"I'm…" I backed up more, obeying the instinct to run. I was sick of running, but I couldn't deny the innate need to be safe. If these women were conning my sister, if this was a setup or sting or something to capture Eva, I couldn't risk being taken again.

"Sonya? Listen, just calm down and—"

"No." I shook my head, backing up faster until I could turn and sprint toward the exit. I couldn't be impulsive like this. I couldn't rush up to the first sighting I had of Eva.

I needed more information. I had to approach Eva in a safe setting, not dart out and act like I was a part of her world. For all I knew, she could be in danger already and I'd make it worse barging in.

"Stop that woman! Stop her!"

Tuning out the security men shouting at me, I concentrated on getting the hell away. Slight pain shot up from my heel again, but I dug in and dismissed it as I barreled past the hostess. A shove at a push bar opened a door back by the kitchen. Leaving all the alarmed shouts and yells from the kitchen staff behind me, I burst out into the alley.

I didn't stop there. With the restaurant security chasing after me, I ran into the back entrance of the adjacent business, uncaring that the seedy strip club would have to be my next best place to hide for now.

8

BEN

I agreed to kill O'Malley purely because it was an excuse to stay in touch with Lev and the other Baranovs. All I wanted was information about Sonya, but they weren't talking about her at all.

I listened in where I could, which wasn't often because my visits to the mansion where Lev waited for updates from me were infrequent. I didn't ever check in with whoever contracted me for a kill. There was no point. I didn't need guidance and hand-holding. I was told who the target was and I eliminated them. End of story.

Besides, whenever I did stop by the mansion, Lev and the other upper men of the family didn't talk about Sonya. I couldn't ask, either, because they'd made it clear they wouldn't reveal a single thing about her until I killed O'Malley.

If I were to ask, that would risk their wanting to know why I was so curious. And I couldn't admit that I'd slept with her. If they were this protective and possessive of their women, they'd be pissed at the liberties I'd taken with one of their own.

All I could do was kill O'Malley first. Then I'd be hired to find Sonya, and they'd give me more clues.

Unfortunately, O'Malley wasn't such an easy target. He was never alone, never off the grid, and I bet the bastard was paranoid to always have someone with him out of fear of someone taking him out.

Following him around, I noticed a pattern. He went from one place to another for meetings, but through my long-distance lens, I had ample evidence of him visiting colleagues and lobbyists to snort coke and laugh. A couple of times, while his "assistants" stood outside the closed door of a hotel room, he'd let hookers entertain him.

O'Malley was just another typical corrupt politician, hard to kill when he was so guarded and hidden.

Who he kept as company hadn't escaped my notice, though.

"He keeps meeting up with Eric Benson," I told Lev one morning when I wanted to "check in".

"I'm not surprised. Where one corrupt lawmaker goes, another follows."

I nodded. I liked that Lev wasn't stupid enough to argue everything he heard. Acting as the leader in Oleg's place for this period, he proved that the whole family was one step ahead, always aware of what was going on out there on the streets.

"They meet up mostly to talk about arranging trafficking routes once they are both sworn in to power in their new positions."

Lev nodded. Vik and Rurik were also in the office, since those three seemed to be something like a team.

"If not for trafficking, then for drugs," Vik said.

After I left their place, I checked the tracker I'd placed on one of O'Malley's cars and followed wherever he was headed. It came as no surprise that the former cop-turned-governor-elect was visiting a strip club again. He was either a pervert or a faithful customer of Viagra pills.

Inside the club, I kept my distance but maintained a view of my target. Like every other time I spotted his pudgy face and got near enough to witness his coming and goings, he was flanked by two beefy guards. I could take them on, but there was always the pesky matter of witnesses.

Eric Benson greeted O'Malley near the hallway that led off to private rooms. It'd be impossible to get into a room if they moved their "meeting" into one of them, but I was in luck. Both men sat at a low table that was positioned off to the side of the large room where music thudded, alcohol was consumed, and naked women danced and showed off their bodies.

Here we fucking go again.

Eric and O'Malley had met up at a strip club five times already this week. I wasn't sure if they thought it made their conversations more of a secret or if they were both that desperate to see a pair of tits. Each time I followed O'Malley and found him at a club with the younger man, they talked about those trafficking routes. Sure, they spoke in a code, but I got the gist of it as I read their lips from a distance.

Keeping my focus on the two men talking, I grew bored, knowing I probably wouldn't have a chance to get close enough to kill O'Malley. It wouldn't be hard to get my gun out and just shoot at him, but again, I'd have witnesses. I'd considered using a sniper rifle, but that didn't seem wise either. The asshole was *always* covered. I'd have to shoot through a guard.

As I sat there and watched them talk, my thoughts wandered again to these Mafia Families who were interested in these politicians. If it were up to the Petrovs or the Ilyins, these guys would be allies, but to the Baranovs, they were nuisances to deal with.

It all seemed so stupid, the grudges and wars. If Igor or the Ilyins succeeded in ending the Baranovs, it wouldn't make them invincible. Both of those families would still ruin themselves one way or another.

I couldn't help but imagine those two families killing each other off. If that were to happen, it wouldn't be a challenge to side with the Baranovs.

Lev was a hard ass, but he treated me fairly. All the men seemed decent, as decent as they could be as killers and criminals. I'd heard about Vik helping Irina Petrov and saving her brother. Just like I'd heard more about Rurik saving Kelly. I'd prefer to stick with people like them instead of idiots like Igor or an Ilyin. I would never be able to stop killing. It was part of who I was, but it'd be nice to continue that vocation with the Baranovs' alliance than without it.

Eric ordered another drink, and I sighed. They were really settling in here. O'Malley seemed more interested in the dancers while Eric seemed to search for something to say about their slight argument over money and campaign donors.

Before I could groan at how much longer I might need to sit here and spy on them, a blur of someone running by snagged my attention.

"What the…" I furrowed my brow, turning my head in the direction of where the person had rushed by. In a dark shirt and tight jeans, the woman sprinted with an athletic grace. She moved with the desperation of escaping, too, and I was instantly curious.

What's going on?

This club was a shithole, but there were security guards hanging around here with the purpose of keeping business running smoothly.

I sat up, following the woman as she collided with a server bringing drinks out to the guests. The tray in the server's arms wobbled, and drinks spilled.

"What the hell?" She scowled at the woman cutting through the room. The brunette turned slightly, stopping herself from falling from the collision.

In that blip of time, in that second of her facing more my way, I saw her.

Her.

It was Sonya.

Months had passed since I saw her, but I was confident. It was her! The same long brown hair, those plump lips and smooth skin. Her slender physique and sharp gaze.

Sonya?

It made no sense why she would be running through here, of all places. Of all times, she'd happen to be here when I was?

Shooting to my feet, willing it to really be her, my feet moved of their own violation. I had to reach her. I had to make sure my eyes weren't playing tricks on me.

Walking after her as she continued down the hallway, further rushing through here as if someone were chasing her, I didn't tear my gaze off her for a second. Locked in on her brown hair swaying as she hurried away, I dropped into a jog after her.

Sonya?

It was on the tip of my tongue to call out for her, but I refrained, following her as she wove around other people coming out of private rooms.

She slipped into one, and I closed the distance between us, intent on cornering her and figuring out why the hottest one-night stand of my life was a vision like this, slipping in and out of my life in the most mysterious pattern.

9

SONYA

I shut the door to a small room and tried to catch my breath. The mad rush from the restaurant next door to this club was nothing but a dizzying blur of panic. But I was alone here. Wheezing and gasping to catch my breath, I waited for my heart to slow. Ever since I realized I had to be pregnant, it was too easy to be winded and lose my breath. After a chase like that—

Behind me, the door opened again. It hadn't been shut for more than a few seconds before someone entered.

Shit!

I backed up, cornered, and confused about who was coming in. The tall man who entered wasn't wearing the black suit the security personnel sported next door. He wasn't someone pursuing me for trying to tell that Petrov girl to stay away from my sister. So many things didn't add up. I only knew I needed to hide and wait, to strategize my return and not be impulsive when things remained unknown to me.

But this guy…

He turned after closing the door behind himself.

This guest had to be someone here for the purpose of being entertained by the dancers.

But it was *him*. Ben. My one-night stand who'd shown me so much pleasure.

My baby daddy.

I narrowed my eyes, still breathing so hard. I couldn't dare to believe it. I had to be imagining things, projecting my memory of him onto others.

Is it him?

His eyes were the same. I hadn't forgotten those deep, dark pools that had shone with raw desire that night. They'd sparkled with mischief and daring too.

But it also wasn't him. His hair wasn't the same. He had glasses on. The facial hair was different.

Is he wearing a disguise?

Or is this someone else?

I opened and closed my mouth, at a loss for what to say. So stunned to see him again, here like this, when I was in the middle of trying to reclaim some privacy, I couldn't speak.

"Um…" He lowered his gaze only to drag it back up me slowly, desire lighting up his slow smile. He wasn't acting like he recognized me, and it made me doubt he was who I thought he could be. Maybe it was just some other guy who *looked* like him. "Excuse me, but are you a dancer here?"

What? How could he think that? I was dressed down in borrowed jeans and a sweater, clearly not appearing ready to show off my body. I was waiting for him to say something like *hey, I remember you. We fucked that one time upstate, right?*

"No," I shot back. I wasn't a damn stripper. I was a Mafia princess. And if he could task himself with thinking back to three months ago, I was also the stranger who'd given him her V-card.

"Huh." He stepped forward, still eyeing me like I was his dessert without an iota of recognition.

He's got no clue who I am. The thought blew my mind.

"I was told I could find a little extra... fun in this room with one of the girls who worked here."

What? How? Huh?

I'd rushed in here to hide, not looking where I was going. It'd be just my damn luck that I'd sneak into a room meant for whores to get customers needing a "little extra fun".

"Is that correct?" he asked, taunting me with his lowered voice, so husky and seductive like I remembered.

I started to shake my head, confused, bewildered, but unafraid. As he walked further into the room, trapping me inside, I couldn't bring myself to tell him that he was wrong. That he was mistaken to come into this specific room where I happened to be hiding and try to get a little something from me.

But now that I was near him, close enough to smell his musky, spicy scent and feel the warmth radiating off his hard, hot body, I wanted it too.

Stop. I couldn't seriously be thinking about this. *This is insane. Not now. Not here.* I couldn't begin to understand how our paths were crossing like this, that we were destined to see each other again at all. That night, after I'd slept with him and the Ilyin guards found me again, I dismissed "Ben" as a stranger I'd never encounter again.

But I had. We'd somehow ended up in the same place at the right time.

He doesn't remember me.

Either he'd forgotten me or he was faking it. I couldn't figure out why he was acting like he was a stranger, but it was similar to how we'd come together the last time.

Strangers. Just two people wanting intimacy.

And in the midst of all this danger and confusion swirling in my life since I dared to break away from captivity, I needed it.

Ben grounded me. In the simplest manner, this man *was* something I knew. I was familiar with him. I recalled how he'd felt and the ease with which he'd mastered my body to make me come.

"Sorry. I must be mistaken," he said, shaking his head.

"No." I reached out for him, so torn with what else I could say.

He was mistaken. It was an error to assume I was a stripper or a whore here. He was also incorrect to not recognize me, or to act like he didn't.

But he was right when he thought he could find a little extra fun in this room with me.

Pushed by a crazy need to have him again, I grabbed the front of his shirt and pulled him closer. Keeping my gaze locked on his, I closed the distance between us until he had me in his arms.

This was wildly stupid. I was acting impulsively again with this stranger. Now wasn't the time to kiss him, but I did. This wasn't the place to bring my body flush against his hard chest, but I did.

Gripped with a desperation to feel him again, all of him, I gave up trying to make sense of this moment and took what I wanted, what my body needed.

Maybe it was pregnancy hormones making me uncontrollably horny for any man. Perhaps this was a form of delusion that could strike after the trauma of being held captive, killing a man, and staying on the run.

I didn't know. I didn't want to explain this deep need to feel Ben.

He represented strength and security. He was a representative of comfort and care. In that one night I'd shared with this stranger, I felt so alive and treasured. Valued and protected.

And wishing I could have those things again, I ignored my mind telling me that this was stupid. I dismissed the warnings that I could be making a mistake.

Lines were crossed. A huge misunderstanding had to be at play between us, but it didn't matter. All that could matter was keeping my lips pressed against his, so hard and firm and demanding that I part mine. All I cared about was holding on to him and never letting go.

Every kiss he gave me heated up the desire coursing through me so quickly that I was dizzy under the spell of instant lust. Each grab of his hands on my sides taunted me to race that much faster toward wanting to rip his clothes off.

He growled and grunted, so noisy and feral, just like before. Ben—or whoever he was—didn't merely peck at me with his lips and hug me within his muscled arms.

No, he moved with every inch of his hard frame. Pinning me to the wall, grinding his erection up against me, and slanting his head to the side to further force me into submission under his dangerously addicting kisses.

Oh, yeah.

In his arms, under his lips, I was free again.

Please.

Don't ever stop.

Making out with my baby daddy obliterated all thoughts from my mind. Kissing him back erased all the stress and confusion that plagued me since I'd broken out from that house.

It couldn't be wise to cave to instant desire like this. I wasn't thinking straight—or at all—but I couldn't help it.

I'd missed him.

I'd yearned for him. And as I tugged at his shirt with the least chance of breaking this kiss, I wanted to act on it while I could.

There was no telling if or when I'd ever get to see this man again. I doubted I would. So while I could enjoy the drugging intimacy and rabid lust that he offered me to experience, I would.

"You want—"

I kissed him harder, cutting off his questions. It was obvious what I wanted. I wanted him. Unlike the last time I'd been with him so spontaneously, I wouldn't be the meek virgin.

I recalled the thickness of his cock, in my mouth and deep in my pussy. After I unzipped him and reached into his pants, I wrapped my fingers around that generous girth again.

I remembered the rough friction of his callused hands on my breasts and nipples. Once I yanked at my shirt and encouraged him to get it off me, I moaned at the greedy grip of his hands groping me there again.

My panties were damp, sticky with cream as he aroused me faster and faster. In the back of my mind, I worried whether this could be good for the baby. *Our* baby. The one I had no desire to tell him about when he was going to act like we were strangers. He hadn't noticed my small baby bump and I wasn't about to point it out now.

Too many things remained complicated between us.

But as we shed our clothes, moaning and grabbing for each other in a hurry to fuck, none of it could matter anyway. Reuniting like *this*, as one, was more important. I needed this man in deep, primal ways I couldn't begin to understand.

Naked and shivering under his heated stare, I waited for him to move me toward the chair, the only piece of furniture in the room. He didn't, though. Instead, as he stood there within my reach, his dick jutting out and pointing at me, he raked his hot gaze over me like he wanted to commit me to memory.

He'd done that before, too. That one night, he'd watched me like he never wanted to forget me.

But he had. Or he was pretending to.

"Please," I begged, anxious to stop thinking, stop worrying and just fuck.

After letting out a deep growl of need, he smiled and advanced toward me. He didn't lift me up. Swiftly gripping my arm and spinning me, he urged me to face away from him.

"Please what?" he teased. Kissing my cheek, he leaned over me as he guided my hands to rest on the top of the lone chair. This position had me bending over in front of him, which seemed to be his intention all along.

With my ass in the air, his hard thighs braced behind mine, I was all his for the taking.

"Please. Fuck me."

Fuck me, Ben.

If he was going to act like he didn't know me, I'd do the same. All that mattered was the relief he'd grant me with a hard fuck like before.

"Like this?" he asked, lining up his cockhead at my entrance. Slick and slippery from my arousal, I welcomed the bulbous tip in.

I groaned, giddy and hungry to feel the full stretch of him sliding in and rubbing along my inner walls. I wanted to feel stuffed with his hard shaft. I needed that breath-stealing awe of pressure.

"Yeah," I replied breathily, ready to whine if he wanted me to. "Please."

Setting his hands on my hips, he held me in place to thrust every inch of his thick cock deep inside me. He growled filthy sounds of need as he seated himself, and the naughty noises of pure satisfaction made this all the more hotter.

"Oh, God…" I moaned, uncaring whether anyone heard. Whether anyone found me.

My baby daddy had. This rugged man who wasn't just a *one*-night stand had stumbled upon me again.

As he pulled back and then rammed back in, driving his dick all the way in, I closed my eyes and let all the sensations overwhelm me.

10

BEN

She doesn't know who I am.

I gritted my teeth, staring at her wet entrance as I reared back. Watching my dick reappear, glistening wet with her cream, was nearly my undoing.

Her pussy felt the same. Tight. Hot. Slick. And just fucking perfect, as though she were made for me alone.

Sonya pushed her ass back, meeting me thrust for thrust.

"Fuck, yeah," I muttered, out of breath but loving every torrid second of our second tryst. "Fuck."

I couldn't get enough of my "stranger" like this.

She wasn't as lax this time, following my lead and waiting for my direction. She wasn't a virgin anymore. I'd seen to it. And with a little experience from having done this before, with me, she seemed more confident to take the initiative to show me what she wanted.

For me to go faster. Harder. Deeper. Each time I clutched her hips and dug my fingers into her flesh, I swore she creamed a little more and squeezed me tighter.

She couldn't get enough of this. Of me.

Yet, she refused to acknowledge who I was.

We weren't goddamn strangers. I was aware that she might have struggled to place me at first, with my hair how I liked it, out of the disguise and cover I had been using when I met her in that bar three months ago.

But she had to know it was *me*. She had to realize this cock deep inside her was the same one that had ended her virginity.

When I first entered the room, I noticed the flare of recognition in her eyes. She remembered. She'd reacted, seeing me and making the connection.

But why is she acting like we're just a couple of strangers now?

Can she know that I'm working for her family?

Is there more to her disappearance than what Lev and the others found out?

Is she playing a game? Conning me and everyone else?

Too many questions flogged my brain, but I couldn't slow down or pause to think through any of them. Not with her mewling and panting in front of me, welcoming me deep inside her pussy. Not when she arched her back and made me wish I could see her huge tits swaying and bouncing from the hard thrusts.

It had been a surprise to see her again, but now as I fucked her ruthlessly, relishing the reward of her moans, I was too distracted by desire to want to stop.

After.

We'd talk after I made her come.

There was no way in hell she was getting away from me so easily this time. In my motel room upstate, when we'd slept together again, she'd snuck away when I went to the bathroom. Here in this tiny little space in the club, I'd hold on to her and make sure she cut this shit out about pretending not to know me.

I'd fuck her brains out. I'd flood her cunt with my cum again. And after, I'd be handling the matter of her absence.

"You're gonna come for me—" A deep grunt followed my words, ending my question prematurely, but I was glad I'd caught myself from saying her name. If she wanted to keep up this game of acting like we were still strangers, I didn't want to be the one to slip first.

"Yes. Yes!" She hung her head lower, tensing under my hands. Crying out loudly, she announced her orgasm at last. I felt it in the squeezes of her pussy around me. I saw it over her trembling skin as it broke out in goosebumps. In the air, the smell of sex grew stronger, and it was just enough to prompt me to follow her into bliss.

Relief streamed through me, making me growl as I thrust twice more. I came with a bold and potent release. Spent and exhausted from the strain of fucking her so fast and hard, I staggered on my feet. My feet arched. My heart raced. My spine stiffened as I emptied my balls and shot deep inside her.

Just like last time, she was perfect. Perfect for me. And I wondered if that could be a possibility once we came down from the high of our releases. Once I talked to her and called her on pretending to not know me, I'd have an answer for why she was trying to hide. I had a hunch it had to tie into the matter of her disappearance, but that wouldn't be an issue anymore.

Now that I'd found her—even if it had been an unexpected discovery —I'd be able to bring her home. She'd be able to explain to all of her family members why she'd been gone for so long.

Deep down in my heart, I wrestled with a slight fear that she might be playing us as fools. If she hadn't been kidnapped or taken but had run away instead, who knew what kind of subterfuge or deception she could be plotting?

What if she ran away from the Baranov home because they were mistreating her? What if she took off because she was being abused or harmed or—

I shook my head, pulling out of her slowly as I watched her slender back.

Easy. Just wait a minute and slow down.

I'd get my answers. I would. But I wanted her to face me as she talked.

She remained leaning over, gasping and shivering from the effects of coming so hard. Her knuckles had turned white with her steadfast grip on the top of the chair. But after I stepped back and watched my cum dribble out of her, I leaned over to remove her hands from the chair and encourage a little more blood to circulate through them.

She stood, clumsy and lax. Leaning against me, she heaved out a deep breath and blinked.

"Can you stand?" I asked, rubbing her upper arms and keeping her upright. A ridiculous smile tore at my lips. She was adorable like this, sleepy and dazed. Fucked thoroughly.

We had a lot to talk about. I needed to get to the bottom of her disappearance. But I couldn't deny she was so damn sexy and enchanting like this.

All because of me. I felt like a king to have this much impact on her. And I couldn't wait to do it again.

"Stand?" She shrugged as she nodded but added, "No."

I chuckled, amused by how endearing she could be all lopsided and sated like this. She didn't have a ton of experience, not if she'd only recently lost her virginity to me. But I was thrilled that *I* had been the one to claim that feat.

What the fuck is with this possessive shit? I couldn't stop myself from wanting to be attached to her, but we had a discussion to get through. She had to explain why she was acting like we were strangers, why she was here in the first place, and what happened that she was estranged or missing from her family.

I had to keep my wits about me with her.

She blinked and rubbed her face as she stepped toward the back of the chair. Propping her hip to it, she slowly lowered to grab her pants and panties that remained caught at her ankles. I hadn't fully gotten my clothes off either. I tugged my pants back up, then retrieved her shirt, then mine.

Without making eye contact, she took her sweater. "That was…" She hesitated to finish her comment as she put her cami shirt on, then worked on getting her arms through the sweater sleeves.

I watched her profile as she stayed slightly facing away from me, wondering what adjective she'd land on.

Hot?

Fast?

Addicting?

Not enough?

"Unexpected," she admitted.

"It was," I said, curious how she meant that word. Unexpected as in she hadn't counted on seeing me again? Or unexpected as in we'd just crashed and fallen into each other and wound up fucking like wild animals?

As I watched her get her clothes back on, I waited for her to speak up again. She wasn't leaving me again, not without some explanations, but I wanted to see if she'd break her silence first. Seconds turned into minutes, and the awkward lack of conversation stretched between us. In the distance, the heavy thud of the music beat on, but it was dim and dulled, not preventing us from talking in here.

"Are—"

Gunfire cut through the quiet in this private room she'd darted into.

She flinched, then stiffened at the second round of shots being fired, but I didn't wait. Diving forward, I covered her body and made sure that if anyone was shooting in the direction of the closed door, the bullet would hit me, not her.

"Get down!" I ordered as shouts and more gunfire erupted outside our room.

"I am down," she retorted. Without moving too far from my body blocking her in case anyone came in here, she fidgeted as though she wanted to keep her distance from me. Which didn't make sense. I'd just been as close to her as a man could get with a woman.

"Stay—" I didn't get a chance to tell her to stay put and stick with this position behind me.

The door opened as someone slammed into it, but no one fell into our space. A fight had ensued out there, and I didn't want our door to remain open. I was armed. I already had my gun in my hand, but I had no clue what was going on out there. My firearm would be used to keep us safe, nothing more.

"You're in my way," Sonya insisted as she wrestled past me, half-crawling and half-running. "Let me out of here. I'm not hanging around when all hell's breaking loose!"

"Wait." I lurched forward, diving to grab her before she escaped and ran through the strip club with who knew how many guns being fired. "Stop! S—"

She kicked back at my hand, making me lose my almost-grab on her. Then with one knee on the ground, she spun and then shot to her feet.

"Stop!" I ran after her, keeping my gun at the ready, but she was already sprinting down the hallway. She was lucky she chose to run away from the bigger, main room where the gunfire seemed to be coming from, but two men fighting blocked me from chasing her.

"Fuck!" I ground my teeth, so frustrated and livid that she'd gotten away.

It wasn't only a pain that she had succeeded, that she'd managed to evade me.

But why?

She wouldn't run away unless she was scared and had a damned good reason to want to hide.

What the hell is your story, goddammit?

What are you hiding?

Who are you trying to screw over, Sonya?

I'd have to wait for answers. She was gone. Already, cops, security guards, bouncers, and bodyguards were settling down the chaos out in the main room.

Pocketing my gun and easing off to the side, I filed into the line of guests who were panicking about guns being fired. Management from the club herded servers, dancers, and guests away from the thick of the fight. I blended in with the mass, making sure I wore a slightly confused and alarmed expression so I'd look like just one more frightened guest among the others.

Before I could be excused—or slip away—I caught enough of what everyone was saying to piece together the story. It sounded like someone had come in to fire at Eric Benson, who was surrounded by members of law enforcement. He lived. Others insisted that the shots were fired at O'Malley, who was shouting and raging at the club manager. He also lived.

Both of those claims were one and the same. Eric and O'Malley had been seated at the same table, so a shot taken at one very well could've been a shot aimed at the other. As soon as the first sound of gunfire had happened, others got their guns out and fired at where they thought the perp was. It was the perfect chaotic storm for too many guns to be fired in too small of a place, hence the general confusion and danger that had taken over the whole place.

What, someone else is trying to take a hit on my target now?

Lev contracted me to kill O'Malley, and I would. But I'd be damned if someone else tried to pull off that feat before I could.

After it seemed like there was nothing else to learn or overhear, I watched Eric and O'Malley exit. Guards and cops flanked them, and I knew their security would be ramped up after this.

Now it'll be even harder to get a lock on O'Malley.

I left, scowling as I headed out of there. I'd just come from the Baranovs' place, but I planned to speak with them again. Updates were a decent excuse to get closer to them, and I sort of had one now. Others might succeed in killing O'Malley before me if those shots had been intended for him, not Eric. But they didn't know that the Ilyins planned to marry Sonya off to him.

Which is not going to fucking happen.

I huffed, finding the thought a joke.

Now that I'd had her, twice, I refused to entertain the idea of some slick politician having the woman who seemed so perfect for *me*.

Secrets and all, Sonya felt like mine.

But before I could let her in on that concept, I had to sleuth around a bit more. Not only to know why she was hiding and staying distant from her family, but also how I could get her to stay and come back.

Once wasn't enough.

Twice wouldn't do either.

There was something about that woman that was twisting me all up inside. She'd captured my attention. If I wanted to be poetic about it, I could admit that just seeing her twice, she'd put a damn spell on me—whether I wanted her to or not.

11

SONYA

This time, when I ran again, I made sure not to stop until I'd put more distance between me and that restaurant. And the strip club where my not-so-one-night stand returned to my life.

Rain fell again. The fall of frigid drops seemed never-ending. While I cursed how soggy this spring was, it didn't prevent me from getting a room at a seedy-looking, rundown hotel near Brooklyn.

With a lockable door and running water in an attached small bathroom, this room was an upgrade from my former lodgings, where I was stuck in captivity on that Ilyin property. A phone sat on the table, but I had no numbers or contacts to call. A mini fridge hummed under a crooked counter that doubled as a TV stand, but I had no food to put in there.

The cash I stole from the Petersons was all but depleted. In the two days that I stayed in this room, trying to catch a break and think out my next steps, I used it all up. The room wasn't cheap. I had a strong hunch the clerk was gouging me on the price, but I couldn't control that. Without an ID, without a credit card, without *anything*, I was stuck paying under the table for this dump.

All the protein and breakfast bars were gone. The apples too. Keeping one water bottle to refill saved me some money, but the water seemed brown when it ran from the faucet.

It's not enough. I had to care for this new life growing in me. My baby —Ben's baby—needed more nourishment.

Prenatal vitamins would have to wait. Whole meals would be coming eventually. Milk. Water. A balanced diet intended to foster a healthy infant. Those were the things that I needed right now. But they'd have to wait.

On the evening of another long, restless day, I suffered through a nagging tension headache and sluggishly paced through the room. Back and forth, I walked and aggravated my sore ankle. Moving was better than sitting, though. Staying upright helped with this nausea that I hoped was a sign of morning sickness—or rather, all-day-and-night sickness. If I was coming down with something, I wouldn't be able to find help.

It seemed so stupid to be in the city but not go home, yet I now knew I had to do this carefully. I had to be deliberate about my return because it seemed I was clueless about whom to trust.

Why would Eva be near that Petrov woman? She wouldn't willingly associate with the enemy, so I had to go with the assumption that she had been taken, or manipulated… or something.

How did that other woman recognize me? I'd been absent for eleven years. I had no idea who she was, and if she'd remembered me from before, I looked different now.

Rubbing my stomach as hunger pangs made me dizzy, I sighed. *I am different now.* I was an expectant mother, wrought with panic, paranoia, and trauma.

I couldn't walk up to the Baranov house when no one would be there, and that was my biggest fear. If Eva was near that Petrov, maybe she had been moved elsewhere. My mother and father were gone. My uncle, too. For all I knew, the mansion I'd once called home could be vacant now or taken by rival families.

"Those bastards," I growled as I rubbed my face. "Those fucking Ilyin bastards." They'd deprived me of any news, any information, and I felt too nervous to reenter society being this ignorant and clueless. How could I know whom to trust or where to go now?

I'd trusted my body with Ben, but in hindsight, I felt so stupid to have wasted time on having sex with him again. It had happened so suddenly, but that was no excuse. Now wasn't the time to let my desires rule me.

Still, as I left my room, I analyzed how that man *had* made me feel so good and comforted. While I was sheltered in captivity for too long, I doubted that the phenomenon that pulled me to him could be normal. I was a level-headed, survivalist kind of woman. Not a needy, clingy idiot.

Then again... I rolled my eyes at the possibility of my hormones wreaking havoc on me.

Okay. Fine. But that's still no excuse.

I refused to waste any more time on sex or even thinking about the sexy man who was fond of playing games with me. He'd recognized me but acted like he didn't, and that was too fishy, too suspicious for me to want to trust him at all, should I see him again.

Needing answers, I headed to a nearby diner that used to be owned by the Petrov family. The crappy hotel I was staying at was more or less on neutral ground. If anyone claimed that neighborhood, it'd be a gang or someone else, not Mafia. Then again, I doubted turf lines had remained exactly the same as what I remembered eleven years ago.

Regardless, I recognized this part of the city. With a hoodie as a way to hide my face, I hoped that entering this specific diner would bring me closer to a member of the Petrov family—another from a Mafia organization. I had to eavesdrop and listen in to get an idea of what had been happening lately. If my memory served me well, men liked to talk at bars, diners, and cafés like this, where they could relax and shoot the shit.

I wasn't disappointed. Up at the counter, a few Petrov soldiers were eating a late meal, talking and laughing freely. They sat up on the stools, carrying on without a care, and I slid onto the booth seat near them while I busied myself with a single cup of coffee. It was all I could afford at this rate, and it would give me a prop to be here for the sake of listening in.

"If I see one of those fucking idiots again, I'll kill them," one man boasted.

I almost rolled my eyes. *Yeah, yeah, Yeah, yeah.* It didn't matter that I'd been gone for eleven years. Some things simply never changed. These soldiers were riled up and annoyed. The threats of killing others didn't faze me. But I was disappointed that they were talking about another organization outside the Mafia circle. I wanted to know about my family, about what remained of the Baranovs so I could return to them and provide for my baby.

"I see you."

I didn't flinch as the young feminine voice reached my ears. Not looking away from my coffee as I idly stirred my spoon in the liquid, I tried to puzzle out who'd spoken.

"I said I can see you," she repeated, haughtier.

Now that I was paying attention for someone to speak up, I tracked her location. Next to me, on the other side of a partition, was a young teenager. I slowly glanced at her, careful not to let any expressions show on my face.

"I see you listening in." The girl who didn't look mature enough to be considered an adolescent smirked at me. "You're spying on them." A tip of her chin toward the counter was all the indication she wanted to show me.

"Excuse me?" I asked, feigning confusion and innocence.

"You've been sitting here spying and listening to what those men say. I'm gonna tell my daddy that you're spying."

I licked my lips, peeved that this scrap of a spoiled child could try to threaten me. After all I'd gone through? After all I'd survived, I had to contend with her acting like this?

"You shouldn't be so cruel," I advised, keeping the heat out of my tone the best that I could. Even though she was young, she could quickly gather attention and cause trouble for me. She could stand up and tell others a stranger was spying here, and I'd be stuck.

She smiled devilishly at me.

"Women need each other's help in this world," I said, thinking back to Jenny's compassion and selflessness. What a contrast she was to this punk.

The girl huffed. "In my world, I don't need help. I'm a princess."

"A Mafia princess?" I asked knowingly.

She tipped her chin up. "Yeah. And I'll never need help. Like my daddy says, I'll never want for anything."

"Oh?" I didn't care that my hood fell back a bit. I wanted to see her fully, and I wanted her to see me while I set her straight. Someone had to explain how things worked in our world. "Is that what you think?"

"That's what I know," the girl sassed.

"Then as one Mafia princess to another, take this advice freely." I licked my dried lips then cleared my raw throat. "You'll want for freedom."

She furrowed her brow.

"You'll be forced to marry a horrible man. You'll be arranged in marriage to some asshole stranger. And you will never be able to make a choice of your own."

"That's..." She frowned and shook her head. "That's not true. My daddy says I'll always be his little girl."

I shook my head. "You're a pawn. Just like me, like all of us daughters in the Mafia, you are a *thing* to be used and sold and traded off."

"I don't..." She lowered her head more. As she seemed to absorb what I said, her spirits sank and her expression turned more troubled. "I thought that was just something people say to scare me into obedience."

Yeah, obedience that your husband will expect one day.

I hated to give her such a blunt reality check, but she would do well to be informed sooner than later. "It's true."

"How do you know?" She scowled, getting defensive and doubtful.

"Because I'm a Mafia princess too."

She studied me the best she could with my hood still partially on. "I don't recognize you. You're not from the Family."

"Not this one." I tapped my finger on the tabletop, indicating the Petrov-owned diner. "But the Baranovs."

She lowered her gaze again, seeming puzzled instead of shocked. This girl was too young to be aware that one of the Baranovs had been taken so long ago. She couldn't possibly understand my return to the city, and that was why I felt safe to divulge my name. If she were to tell her daddy that I was here, he probably wouldn't believe her.

I watched her, letting her sit with this advice, but I disliked the pain I felt for her to accept the truth. All of us women suffered the same ugly fate.

Married off. Bred. And dismissed. That was how most Mafia families operated, but not the Baranovs.

Because being owned like that was no life.

Even though most of my family was gone, I refused to let Eva be trapped in a hopeless existence. And it wasn't the life I wanted for the baby in my belly, either.

I huffed. "I wish I could've been around to act like a big sister to my sister," I mumbled to her, knowing this spoiled girl wouldn't care.

"Has she been forced away to a horrible man?" the girl asked.

"I haven't been in the city lately, but I plan to make sure Eva will never be—"

Her brows shot up. "Eva?"

Shit. I didn't like that spark of recognition that showed on her face. I felt safe enough to tell her who I was because I doubted she'd understand the significance behind my presence. But she clearly had heard of Eva.

"Eva Baranov is already married," the girl stated.

I frowned, instantly suspicious that she was messing with me.

"She chose her husband," she added.

Eva's already married? It was too far of a stretch of the imagination to believe it. "Eva Baranov is married?" I asked.

"Yeah, she—"

One of the men turned from the counter, ordering her to come and leave with him. While she was replying to her father, I lowered my head, pulled the hoodie back up over my face, and slid out of my seat.

Too close. Too much attention. I had to get out before she pointed me out or tried to alert anyone there about a Baranov princess being in their presence.

Too many questions.

I'd gone there to learn something—anything—about my family's situation that I was returning to.

All I'd discovered was that it was too late to save my sister from being a pawn for another man or family.

Eva was already married.

That girl claimed that Eva had chosen her husband, but until I could see my sister in the flesh, I had no way to guess whether she was trapped.

12

BEN

The day after I encountered Sonya at that strip club, I finally got close to the Baranovs again. With Oleg in the hospital still, his closest confidantes would be there too. It wasn't easy to merely ask for permission to come up to that floor and into his private room. They'd insisted on layers of security while their leader was vulnerable.

That didn't stop me, though. Another disguise, this one as a member of the janitorial staff, got me into Oleg's room.

Once more, I was privy to spying on them and listening in.

I couldn't shake the possibility that Sonya was reluctant to return to her family. Details were missing, but I didn't want to dismiss the idea that I'd be doing my flaky lover a disservice to bring her home.

Lev and Vik sat at the table in the room. While I did intend to talk to them, observing and listening to them first seemed wiser.

They weren't alone.

Oleg slept on, still and linked to tubes and wires on the bed. Near the table where Lev and Vik sat, women joined them. Rurik paced near the windows as his wife shook her head at him.

"Rurik, I swear I saw her."

Rurik glanced back at her. "You've never seen her before."

Kelly shook her head, frowning at Eva, who sat on Lev's lap. She stared at Oleg sleeping, a worried expression etched on her face.

"I know that," Kelly replied, "but based on knowing what Eva looks like, I swear it was Sonya."

Yes! Elation filled me that they were talking about her. I'd snuck in here at the right time.

"She was at the restaurant, asking why Irina was there. She kept calling out for Eva after she walked away from the table to go to the restroom," Kelly insisted.

"At Mancy's?" Lev asked, glancing at Eva.

She nodded. "Yes. We had lunch there."

And Mancy's was right next to that strip club. Things were piecing together little by little. Sonya must have been running from the restaurant and cut through the strip club.

"But it couldn't have been Sonya, Kel." Eva winced, skeptical as she looked at her new cousin-in-law. "Sonya ran away because she didn't want a life in the Mafia."

Whoa. Is that true?

So far, I'd gotten the impression that some people had forgotten that Sonya existed. Some seemed to believe she was dead. Now, I grappled with the idea that some predicted she could've run on her own.

Which is it?

Because if I intended to see Sonya again and keep her in my life for more than intermittent quickies when we crossed paths, I'd need to know.

"She didn't run away," Rurik argued. "She was kidnapped. You know this."

Eva crossed her arms. "That's what we were led to believe."

"But your mother disappeared with her," Lev reminded her.

"Yes. My mother wanted out of the Mafia life too." Eva stood, apparently too upset to sit still. "My mother was sick of my father being unloyal to her. She left after he knocked up Igor's wife and had that boy. My mother wanted out, and she took Sonya with her. Leaving *me* stuck here."

"Stuck?" Lev asked gently with a small smile. "You feel stuck in a horrible life here?"

She sighed, sitting on his lap again. "Well, not anymore. Now that I've got you..."

"But that's not all," Kelly said, interrupting the lovey-dovey couple. "It *was* Sonya. She called Eva her sister, ergo, she had to be Sonya. And she was pregnant."

I froze.

I couldn't move with that news.

Pregnant?

I furrowed my brow and zoned out, staring at the floor.

She's pregnant?

I would've known. I'd fucked her. I'd touched her. We'd been together for too short of a time in that little room, but dammit, I would've noticed *that*. As I thought back to that hot, brief tryst, I realized how I might not have been aware.

It had been dimly lit. She'd kept herself turned away from me. I'd taken her from behind.

Oh, shit...

My pulse raced as I connected another thought to this bombshell.

"It wasn't that obvious," Kelly said, her voice almost sounding like it was far away with the rush of blood roaring in my ears, "but I saw her bump. She's pregnant."

Stunned, I tried to talk myself out of the assumption that rocked my world.

If Sonya was pregnant, it could be my baby. I could've knocked her up that one night upstate.

"Goddammit." Lev's voice sounded too close. As I registered his growl, he smacked the broom out of my hands. So shocked and distracted by what Kelly had shared with them, I ceased moving, just standing there. Lev was sharp enough to notice. I had to have looked like I was listening, not working, and I hated that I'd dropped my guard like that.

"Fucking Warner." He scowled. "Sneaking in to spy on us again? What the fuck?"

I shrugged, shuttering the shock on my face. "Like I told you before, you're a hard man to get ahold of."

He scowled, raking his gaze over my janitor uniform. "If you intend to speak with me, sneaking in and spying to get close isn't a smart way to do it."

I smiled. "What can I say? I'm good at what I do."

"Don't get smug about it." He crossed his arms. "I'm not fond of anyone who tries to sneak close and listen to private conversations."

"It's not that private. You've already explained that you'd like to hire me to find Sonya—"

"*After* the hit on O'Malley," Lev reminded me. "Seriously. You try to spy on us again, I'll kill you myself."

"Then be more forthcoming with information so that I don't have to feel like you're leaving me in the dark."

He scrunched his face, madder yet. "Are you kidding me? What the…" He huffed and shook his head, exasperated. "You're an independent contractor, Warner. You're not privileged to have more information that's intended only for family."

Well, guess what. I might be family already. If Sonya was carrying my baby, then I was affiliated with the Baranovs by blood in an indirect way.

That was an avenue of leverage I didn't want to reveal yet. Not until I knew whether Sonya was pregnant. And if I was the father. Only then would I consider what it could mean to be connected to the Baranovs. At the moment, though, the idea didn't piss me off. I'd much rather ally with them than the Petrovs or Ilyins, if I were going to ally with anyone.

"I wanted to get ahold of you to discuss the O'Malley hit," I said instead, changing the topic from Sonya, now that I could personally have higher stakes in her return.

"Then stop fucking spying," Lev warned. "You want to talk to me, then be upfront and come talk to me."

"Sure, because you make yourself accessible."

Vik frowned at me. "If you have to sneak in to get close, why snoop while you're at it?"

"Because I haven't gotten as good as I am without understanding and respecting the value and wealth of intel."

"So you'll turn on us?" Lev accused, advancing toward me with his fist reared back to punch me.

"No." *That wouldn't make sense if my child might be one of you...* The notion that I could have a child threatened to stun me all over again. I hadn't had enough time to come to terms with this, and I refused to get ahead of myself or let my hopes get up too high until I found Sonya and spoke with her once and for all.

"Again," I said, determined to change the topic, "I intended to get ahold of you and give you an update about the O'Malley hit."

Behind Lev, Kelly winced and folded into Rurik's arms for a hug.

"What is it?" Lev demanded.

"I followed Eric Benson and O'Malley to a strip club yesterday." I glanced at Kelly. "The one next to Mancy's, in fact. And someone else took a shot at them there."

Vik nodded and crossed his arms. "Yeah. We heard about that already."

"While I'm pissed that the fuckers didn't die, I'm not surprised someone else wants them dead," Lev said.

Nor was I. Corrupt politicians were asking for it. If they wanted to play stupid, dangerous games, they'd get what they had coming sooner or later. Eric and O'Malley likely had plenty of enemies.

"I'll keep at it," I promised him.

But I'm going to keep on looking for Sonya, too.

She'd become my priority, and I didn't care whether these Baranovs approved of that change of plans or not.

13

SONYA

Too soon, the nausea took over. I had one night left at the rented room I'd found, and I dreaded having to find another place to stay.

I could try to see if anyone's at the mansion...

Shaking my head as I lay on the lumpy mattress, I heaved out a sigh and rejected that idea.

I'd tried earlier to have someone drive me there. The young woman gave me a side-eye when I said I didn't have a phone and could pay her cash instead—the last of my cash. But when she typed in the address of the mansion, she freaked out and backed away.

"You want me to drive to one of the Mafia compounds?" She scoffed and retreated. "Hell no. Like, no way, girl. I don't want to get involved with that shit, like, at all."

But as I tried to relax on this bed, I wished I could find someone to take me home, if that still was a home.

Being pregnant had to be a challenge to adjust to, but going at it alone sucked. It was a struggle to convince myself that I wouldn't be suffering, and without the bare basics of needs for much longer. Until I could overcome my paranoia about someone hearing about my return and trying to hold me back from getting home, I felt like I was at a personal stalemate.

Maybe... maybe I shouldn't have run from Ben.

I opened my eyes as my stomach growled louder yet, so knotted and clenched with hunger that I feared it'd never stop hurting.

"No," I whispered to myself. "I can't trust him." How could I trust the not-so-unfamiliar stranger when all we had between us was random, spontaneous sex?

And you. I rubbed my stomach, wondering if this touch could be felt by the baby somehow. This little one connected me to Ben, yet that wasn't enough for me to want to run to him, if I even knew how to find him.

He'd pretended not to know me, and that wasn't a great foundation for rekindling or starting a relationship.

He's no one who has to matter. He can't. He's just a stranger I had the fluke luck to see twice.

And to fuck twice.

I winced, regretting that when I should've been thinking with my head and trying to find safety somewhere so I could think and plan my next steps, I'd been caving to carnal desire for him.

Another low and long cramp of hunger hit me, and I curled into more of a ball as I rolled to my side. "What is it?" I whined aloud quietly. "An empty stomach makes me feel sicker?" The urge to vomit hadn't returned, but I wouldn't be so easily duped. "Or a full stomach makes me more nauseous?" I couldn't tell, and I swore this morning or afternoon or night sickness was something that would come and go as it pleased.

Giving up on staying in and waiting out this nausea, I got to my feet and forced myself to go to the nearest convenience mart and grab some peanut butter and bread. It wouldn't be a balanced meal, but it would be more than vending machine junk that didn't fill me.

As I dragged myself out the door, I counted the change and cash I had in my pocket. The irony of being so destitute was getting to me. I was Sonya Baranov, a Mafia princess. If I could figure out how to get home, I would—like that tween said in the diner—want for nothing.

Feeling as tired and weary as I did, I couldn't fathom the headache of either walking to the mansion or convincing someone to drive me there.

Dammit. I had less than I thought. I wasn't sure I had enough to buy anything.

Maybe I could manage the bread *or* the peanut butter, but not both.

In the store, I browsed down the aisles, growing weaker, hungrier, and thirstier by the second. Focusing on the prices became a challenge, and I found myself blinking slower and slower as fatigue gripped me.

After I bumped into a cardboard stand at the end of the aisle twice, I felt the telltale burn of someone's stare on my back. Spinning around, I caught the disgruntled woman behind the checkout counter glaring at me. Her brows were penciled in and arched so high with disdain, she looked villainous as she tracked my movements.

Fuck off.

I was in no mood for someone judging me. She could think I was some poor, wretched fool. She could criticize how unsteady I looked. But I lacked the patience to deal with having to speak to anyone.

A small smile stayed plastered on my face, though, because if I showed my true emotions of annoyance, that would only be fodder for her to dislike me and watch me closer.

Blending in and looking nonthreatening were the goals here. In and out. But dammit, why did there have to be so many different brands and kinds of peanut butter? And the variety of bread? The flavor didn't matter, but I had to count on getting the biggest bang for my buck.

Once more, I stumbled. I took too short of a step over and smacked into the shelving unit. A couple of boxes of crackers fell. When I reached out to grab them before they dropped and the contents cracked, I sent a bag of chips flying off its spot on the rack too.

"Oh, come on," I mumbled, furrowing my brow and trying to wake up so I wouldn't be this clumsy.

"Hey!" The woman at the register rounded the counter and pointed at me. Stern and serious, she glowered at me like I was the worst excuse for a person on earth. "I saw that."

"Huh?" I turned back and forth, looking at the items I'd knocked off to her approaching me. "I'm sorry. I'm putting it all back up and…"

"No! I saw you trying to put those things in your pockets." She had her phone out, already lifting it to her ear for a call.

"*What?*" I scrunched my face. "What things?" I looked down at the big, voluminous bags of chips and crackers. How in the hell could any of this fit in a pocket?

"Don't play dumb with me, girl. I saw you. I've been watching you since you came in here, acting all high and funny."

"I'm not high." I was tired, that was all. How dare she be so rude? I'd bumped into that stuff accidentally.

"Bullshit. You're stealing those snacks and shit. You probably got more things under your shirt."

"What!" I stepped back, bumping into the shelves again. "I am not stealing anything!"

"Don't lie to me!" She kept her furious stare on me as she spoke on the phone. "Yeah. I need to report someone stealing from my shop."

"No!" I put my hands up, trying to stop her from talking. Showing that I had nothing in my pockets didn't change her mind. No matter what I said, how quickly and vehemently I argued with her, she didn't end her call.

"I'm not stealing anything!"

"Tough shit," she snarled. "Convince the cops of that."

No!

The cops wouldn't do me any good. Nowhere was safe for me. I wasn't safe with those Ilyin captors who wanted to force me to marry some Benson man. I wasn't safe out here in the open, with the general members of society with their phones and Ubers and fear of going near the Mafia. And I wasn't safe with the cops either. No member of any Mafia family wanted to deal with law enforcement. That antagonism was mutual, too. They wanted nothing to do with us, either.

If I were caught and taken in, there was no telling which corrupt cop could be in charge. My uncle Oleg used to have a few officers in his pocket, but so much time had passed. Uncle Oleg was dead. I had no knowledge of who could be in charge of the family and which men we could count on looking the other way.

But I was well aware of the possibility of any cops out there being friends with the Ilyins.

"No, please. I didn't steal anything."

The clerk scoffed at me as a pair of cops entered the shop. "Yeah, well with how nervous you're acting, I'll bet my paycheck that you're hiding something!" She snapped her fingers and directed the cops closer. "This is the woman. Over here."

"No. No." I turned to run down the aisle, but the taller officer must have suspected I'd try to flee.

He was faster, catching me in no time. His arms circled me and didn't let go, not as I kicked, flailed, and fought to break free.

"I didn't do anything!" I wiggled and wrestled, not giving up for a second. I couldn't give up. My last stint of captivity was too fresh in my mind for me to go easy on this cop. I would fight and resist until my last damn breath.

"Hold still!" the other cop said as he tried to slap handcuffs on my wrists.

"No!" I fought him too, but with how exhausted I already was, I had no chance of holding them both back.

They didn't pause or listen to me, not letting up until they had me cuffed and ordered me to stop resisting and to settle down as they forced me outside the shop with them.

"Stop them! Let me go! Someone, stop them. Help me!"

But no one did. As I was roughly pushed into the backseat of their car, I clamped my lips shut tight and heaved out angry exhales through my nose.

No one would help me. I was, once again, all on my own.

And I was sick of it.

Panic swept through me, making my heart race and my breaths shallow.

They were taking me further away, and I had no doubt in my mind that they would ultimately deliver me right back to the Ilyins.

I'd be taken to my unwanted fiancé, and I wasn't sure I'd be able to get away a second time.

14

BEN

I'd lost her.

Twice now, I'd lost Sonya. The first time, it was planned. We'd agreed that our one night of her losing her virginity would be a fling. A single incident. Although there was no way I could've counted on how much she would've left a lasting impression on my mind.

The second time, after our quickie at the strip club when she'd rushed through there, she bolted again. That wasn't planned. While we got dressed, I prepared and mentally rehearsed how to bring up so many things—why she was acting like she didn't remember me, why she'd been away from the Baranov family for so long, and how she'd ended up there at all.

Impatient and frustrated, I spent my every minute scouring the city for her.

First, I hacked into the surveillance cameras at Mancy's and at the strip club. They didn't provide me with much. It seemed like she'd gotten into an argument with Kelly and Irina at the table the women had been seated at for lunch, but the view of that section was too distant for me to understand what was said. Per Kelly's explanation to the Baranov men, she was under the assumption that Sonya wanted to separate Eva from Irina, but she was too flighty to stick around and answer anything.

Then, I walked around near the two buildings to see if she came back. That was the bigger waste of my time, relying almost on luck to strike.

Looking for her online didn't get me anywhere either. She was staying off the grid, with no cards being used at all. Interestingly, there was no death certificate filed for her. Some of the Baranovs, like Lev, seemed to have written her off as already dead. If she was, no actual document had been filed anywhere to claim that. Then again, the Mafia had their ways of getting around standard documentation protocols.

I couldn't find Sonya anywhere, and the more that I tried to hunt her down, the more I worried that I was spending too much time and effort searching for her instead of handling the hit on O'Malley.

While Lev had already said he'd hire me to find Sonya *after* I killed the governor-to-be, I couldn't get him to ease up and let me work on the Sonya case at the same time. He clearly noticed how interested I was in looking for her because he stated, "You kill O'Malley first, then you can look for her."

Balancing my priorities, I shifted my schedule to get that old man out of the way. It was easier said than done, though. O'Malley was in the hospital after that strip club shooting, and he had just as many layers of security there as the Baranovs had on Oleg at the other facility.

I couldn't get to O'Malley to kill him at the moment. Guards could be passed or rendered unconscious, but it was the media that I couldn't sneak around. Lots of reporters and cameras were waiting for the next governor to be discharged, but from all that I saw online, rumors were spreading that he didn't even need medical care at all. The word was that O'Malley was acting wounded for pity and to look like a martyr or something like that.

I didn't give up, though. Being idle wasn't my style.

Since I wasn't having any luck finding Sonya and I was limited with ways to hunt for her, I figured I could try to follow some Ilyin men who seemed to be hanging around the hospital where O'Malley was "recovering".

I'd noticed them hanging around there. My first thought was that the Ilyin family had sworn protection to the governor-to-be. That was the only explanation that would fit the circumstances.

However, when I loitered near them, waiting for them to say something about their assignment, I realized I might have been too rash to assume their presence there had anything to do with O'Malley. Neither of the two men who stood near the hospital entrance mentioned the politician.

After a couple of hours of watching them, I deduced this had to be the most boring stakeout I'd ever accomplished.

And it's all a crapshoot anyway. I had no proof to justify that the Ilyin men could be connected to O'Malley at all.

"Yeah?" one of the two Ilyin men said as he answered his phone.

Both of them stalled under the awning of a bus stop stand. I remained further back, undercover as a homeless man begging for money from passersby.

"Yeah, he's with me," the man told whoever had called him. He tipped his head up at his partner, beckoning him to come closer.

The men didn't speak as they listened to the call, their heads bent over so their ears would be within reach. Whatever was said was brief and to the point. And if the shocked and determined expressions on their faces were any indication, they were expected to act.

"Fuck, man." The first one ended the call and put his phone away. "This is fucked up."

"It is," the second guy said, nodding his head. "But let's hurry up and offer backup." He didn't need to tell his partner. The man was already on the move, leaving their post here.

Huh. I wonder what's going on. I fell into step behind them at a distance. Walking briskly, I made sure I wouldn't lose them and so they wouldn't be able to turn around and see me stalking them.

Something was up, though. Something had alerted them into action.

"First, Brant was killed," the first Ilyin said.

"And then Joseph was attacked," his buddy added. "All because that bitch had to try to get away."

I was familiar with a female trying to get away.

But they can't be talking about Sonya, though... Right? I hurried to keep up with them, eager to follow this development.

I didn't see how Sonya could be involved, but it didn't feel like a reach. She was the woman on my mind. She was the lover I was desperate to locate, the one I wanted to make mine after two meetups with her. It made sense that she'd be the first woman to come to my mind, but I didn't like the idea that she could have been escaping from the Ilyins. I didn't care for the idea of anyone trying to hurt her or hold her captive.

It might not be her. They could be talking about anyone. Rage steamed hotter within me at the mere thought, but I tried to tamp down those ideas. Mafia men were notorious for kidnapping others.

"She can try," the second man said, "but she won't get far."

"I bet she'll be spitting mad and fighting even harder now."

The second Ilyin nodded and glanced at him. "She escaped once, but if we hurry up to the safehouse they're taking her to, we'll be able to join in on the lesson of showing her what happens when someone thinks they can fuck with the Ilyins."

Who? Who are you talking about? I hustled up so I wouldn't lose them on this crowded sidewalk full of too many busy pedestrians.

"We'll take that bitch back to where she belongs," the taller one vowed.

"Damn straight," the other said.

I furrowed my brow, dropping into a jog when they headed toward a car. Chasing after them on foot wouldn't be possible now. I had to retreat to where I'd parked.

Pretending to trip on the curb, I bumped against their car and fell, looking like another homeless person.

"Watch it, you filthy motherfucker," one of the Ilyins said, kicking at me while I was down on the pavement. "Goddamn beggars. Get the hell away from me."

I rolled to dodge his boot hitting my face, but before I pretended to struggle getting on my hands and knees, I quickly leaned in to stick a magnetic tracking device on the underside of their car.

Got you now.

They could drive away and I'd have a bead on their path.

Once I groaned and crawled upright, they sped off. I glanced over my shoulder to see if they were out of sight, and then I dropped into a sprint for my SUV a couple of blocks over.

This still might be a dead end. It might be a fool's errand. Maybe they were talking about someone else.

Deep in the pit of my stomach, I felt a sickening hunch that they were racing to get to Sonya and teach her that lesson about running away from them.

Call it intuition. Perhaps I was motivated to follow nothing more than wild speculation. But there was not a chance in hell that I'd stop and reconsider hurrying toward this safehouse—just in case Sonya was the escapee they'd managed to reclaim.

15

SONYA

The second the cops got a good look at me, I knew it was over. Without an ID, without my saying a single word to their questions or speaking up at all, they still knew. Baranovs were royalty in the Mafia circles, and I supposed the family resemblance didn't lie.

"I think it's her," one cop said at the station. He held out his phone, showing another law enforcement member a photo of Eva. They had a file on her, at least a digital one or a photo. In the split-second glimpse I had of her, I knew they were matching me to her.

"It's her sister," the other cop said, raising his brows at me. "But I thought Geoff wanted to have her…"

I slitted my eyes, daring the man to finish his sentence.

Geoff Ilyin wanted to have me marry a Mr. Benson? He kidnapped me and held me until I could marry some dumbass of his choosing? Yeah, that sums it up, you asshole.

"I'll be right back." He smiled and held up his phone. "I'm going to make a quick call."

The first cop who was standing over me in the small, windowless interrogation room grinned. "This is gonna be a sweet payday, right?"

"Fuck yeah. We're getting a bonus for finding her." As the man exited the room, he rubbed his finger and thumb together, gesturing that he counted on lots of money coming to him.

I tuned out all further questions they lobbed at me. I wouldn't tell them my name. I wouldn't tell them where I'd come from. They would get nothing out of me, but I wished I could have the confidence to know that the Baranov family still existed and held power. It was on the tip of my tongue to insist they contact the head of the Baranov family, but I didn't even know who that was supposed to be with my uncle, father, and mother dead.

Besides, they'd made it clear that they were in the Ilyins' favor. There had to be a solid association or expectation between them for these two cops to so readily want to call my captors into the station.

When the one man returned, aiming his phone's camera at me and letting someone see who I was via a video call, it was really over.

"Yeah, that's the bitch," a gruff voice replied. "I'll send some men over to the station to collect her."

Dammit! I bit the inside of my cheek to keep from screaming at them in rage.

They didn't wait to transport me out of the station. It was cruel, how corrupt and evil these supposedly "good guys" were. Police officers were the civilians' heroes. Or they should've been. I bore witness to how wicked and greedy they could be, handing me over to pissed-off Ilyin guards who slapped lots of cash into the cops' hands outside in the back of the station.

On the drive away, I remained closed-lipped and silent. Inside, I was fuming and ranting, shrieking until my throat would've been hoarse if I opened my mouth and released the sounds of pure anger and horror.

Both of the Ilyins talked and joked. They laughed and taunted me, calling me names and promising pain for what I'd done.

I knew I'd killed the one man to escape their property upstate, but I was glad I'd rendered the other man sterile from how I'd fought him to get free.

"We're going to fuck you up before handing you over to Benson," one promised darkly.

"You'll regret trying to get away," the other sneered. "Big mistake."

Fuck you. Fuck you both! Bottling in my fury and panic nauseated me, but I couldn't try to find a rational line of optimism or hope to keep me from vibrating with rage. I felt like a coiled-up, ticking bomb, ready to lash out and explode.

Soon, in a blur with how shocked I was at the rapid sequence of too much action in a short span of time, I spotted a warehouse further from the city.

The Ilyins were rough as they forced me out of the backseat and coerced me into entering the building. Maybe they considered this a safehouse, but I knew what it really was. Cots lined one wall. Pots used for toilets sat next to them. Fortunately, no other occupants were being held here at the moment, but I recognized this building as a halfway stop for where they'd keep or move the children and women intended to be sold into trafficking.

"Don't even think about it," a soldier growled as he lowered to grab my wrists.

I didn't bother to ask what *it* was. With how I'd left them before, killing a guard and severely injuring another, he had to be wary of my putting up a fight again.

To my surprise, he cut the chain of metal links that held my handcuffs together.

Why would you want to—

Then he yanked me up to stand so he could punch me.

No! I realized what he was doing a second before he delivered the strike. His fist reared back, and in that brief beat of time, I had the protective instinct to drop down.

He couldn't hit me like that. Not on my stomach. Nowhere near my baby! Terrified of what I could face here, I let the boiling anger and fierce need to protect my child rule me. I would be a feral, rabid, and uncontrollable mama bear. If they wanted to show me how mad they were that I'd gotten away before, they would *not* harm my baby!

Dropping down ensured that he'd punched my face instead. My head jerked back, and instant agony lanced over my skin.

"You stupid ass," another Ilyin man yelled at him, forcing him back and away from me as I breathed through the pain of the beating. "You can't hurt her where anyone can see! Benson won't want her delivered with bruises."

"I don't give shit. She killed my brother. Benson can have his fucking virgin however she'll look like by the time I'm through with her."

"Dumb cunt," another man said as he kicked my leg.

Again, I curled to protect my stomach. They could try to break me down all they wanted, but they wouldn't get to harm my child.

Over and over, they struck out at me. When they stopped, pausing, one held the others back. They all heaved out harsh breaths, winded from the exertion of attacking me.

"You're—" He wiped spit from his mouth. "You see how she's leaning over?"

"Huh?" One of the others narrowed his eyes.

"She's holding her stomach," the one pointed out. "Are you—Fuck!" He lunged to grab my arm and pull it back. Moving so quickly, he had an advantage in the element of surprise. I wasn't prepared to keep my arm close, and as he yanked it aside, they all could see my small baby bump that I was trying so hard to protect.

Tears streaked down my face, wetting my skin with the scalding liquid, but I'd be damned if I wasted the time to wipe them away. Pain filled me. Every cell of my body seemed to be lit on fire with inflammation. But my priority was to wrap my arms around my stomach again.

"She's not a virgin anymore!"

"Someone knocked her up?"

"We're supposed to give him a virgin."

"How the hell did this happen?"

They shouted and cursed, freaking out with their voices overlapping each other's in a frantic flurry of anger and shock.

"You stupid fucking bitch!" the leader of them roared. "You're not taking some bastard baby to your fiancé. You hear me?" After stepping aside, he returned with a crowbar. "Your little bastard isn't going to fuck up the plans. You're going to marry Benson, but not with someone else's bastard in your belly."

As he reared the crowbar back, as if to swing it like a bat at me, two others grabbed my arms and held them back. With my stomach thrust out, the sadist had a clear shot to strike my belly.

"No!" I screamed it until my face stretched with the force of straining my face so hard. "No!" I kicked and bucked, flailing and fighting to break free with every last reserve of my energy. "Don't!"

"Shut up, you whore," the man warned, a nefarious snarl curling his lips. "Shut up and pay for your sins." He lifted his arms again, the metal rod lined up to come into contact with me.

But then a hole showed on his brow. A single dot, clean and small. Blood rimmed the new spot.

Stunned immobile, he stared ahead, not down at me. His arms began to lower as he pitched forward.

Someone had shot him. Someone had come to help? Someone—

I wrenched to the side the best I could, craning my neck to see who was behind us.

Ben.

He'd come. He was *here*.

Somehow, my baby daddy, my mysterious man, had come here to shoot my attackers.

"Get him!" The Ilyin holding my right arm released me to reach for his gun, but Ben was faster. Moving his arm, he aimed and fired again, taking out that man. And again for the man who'd gripped my left arm. Then another man fell as more ran into the fight.

One by one, shots were fired. Ben was picking them off cleanly. Calm and poised, he shifted his arms and shot the Ilyins as they filed out into the room.

Ben.

Ben was *here*.

Just when I'd feared the worst horror ever, being unable to protect my baby, he'd shown up.

Right at the moment when I knew I'd never survive the loss of my child and get over the pain of this beating, he strolled in to save the day.

Before I could accept the cruel reality that I'd been captured again, he'd changed my fate.

I couldn't understand any of it—why he was here, how he'd known to come, and when he'd targeted me as the woman he needed to rescue.

Questions stabbed my mind, but they didn't settle with the dizzying cloud of shock that enveloped me.

Sinking down, curling over as I hunched to the ground, I closed my eyes and waited for it all to stop. Leaning over like this, in the tightest ball I could manage, was my last line of defense for my baby.

Our baby.

He wasn't just saving the stranger he'd fucked twice now, but also the new life he'd helped create in me.

Plastered low to the floor, I hugged my stomach. I clenched my eyes shut tight, willing no stray bullets to reach me as the Ilyins and Ben completed their shootout.

I didn't understand any of this, how he, of all people, had come to save me.

I couldn't try to figure it out, not yet. All I could do was hold on and wait for the all-clear that we would be alive after all this carnage and death.

16

BEN

I shot the man who wanted to attack Sonya with a crowbar. He dropped dead.

Then I shot the men holding her back. Both fell before they could reach for their guns.

I killed them all. One by one, the Ilyin Mafia men filed into the room, lured by the commotion. And I ended each one of the bastards.

I didn't think. I didn't feel. I moved on autopilot, numb to any distractions in this war. All those times in combat in the military had honed me into this machine of death. My hits were solitary tasks, carefully planned out and executed.

This was a massacre, and I didn't stop until every single one of them was dead.

More will come.

I knew that. This wasn't a game over moment just because I'd moved with precision and professional accuracy to shoot all ten of these men before they could get a reliable shot at me. Someone would be alerted further back from another part of this building. A camera could be watching. These Mafia families didn't leave shit to chance, so I knew, without a doubt, this window of opportunity to flee with Sonya wouldn't last.

"Get up." Keeping my gun at the ready and scanning my surroundings, I ran up to Sonya curled up on the floor. She was hunched over, covering her belly, but she was alive. Bruised, bloody, and shaking, but alive.

"Sonya. Get up. Let's go." I couldn't soften my voice. I wasn't able to lighten up and coax her into rising off the filthy floor. This was the time for orders. For strategy. For getting the fuck out of here while we could.

I reached for her sleeve as she slowly began to lift up. Blinking her big, dark eyes, she showed me a bewildered gaze as she checked her surroundings. More and more, she leaned up, but this wasn't the time to dawdle. She could react and freak out later. Right this instant, we had to move it.

"Come on. Let's go!" I held onto her arm with a tighter clutch, helping her to stand and also to pull her along with me.

She didn't protest. Maybe she was too shell-shocked to process what was happening or that she still lived. Tucked into the middle of a shootout, it *was* a miracle she hadn't been shot. And she wasn't. On her feet, her legs shaky as she found her stride, she moved without any suggestion of a gunshot wound.

"Come on," I urged, still using a voice of command to push her to hurry as fast as she could. Any second now, an Ilyin could show up and try to stop us. I was half tempted to pick her up and carry her, to rush faster, but I had to keep at least one hand available to shoot if I had to.

No one came at us as we ran for my SUV idling outside the building, and I exhaled a slight breath of relief that Sonya was too dazed to protest. Or maybe she trusted me because I'd killed those men to spare her life.

Now wasn't the time to figure out the reason for her motivation to go with me, but the second she was in the passenger seat and I shoved the gear stick into drive, I appreciated that she hadn't put up a fight, argued, or wanted to ask any questions.

This was a matter of life or death, and she was in agreement to come along.

"Are you kidnapping me?" she accused as soon as I sped further from the warehouse.

"No." I reached over to shove at her head, though. "Get down!"

Gunshots were fired, and the pings of the shots on my bullet-proof windows followed. Two cars zoomed close, giving chase, and I focused on speeding away without crashing. All the while, Sonya tucked down and ranted at me, bitching me out for daring to think I could be the next one to kidnap her.

"I'm not—" I cut myself off with a growl as I turned sharply to lose the car after us. They crashed into a building, and I checked on the location of the other car.

"Then where do you think you're taking me? Against my will."

"For fuck's sake. You want to live, don't you?" I gritted my teeth to get the SUV turning even sharper the other way. The car in hot pursuit after us couldn't keep up, and they slammed into a truck at an intersection. "I'm taking you to a safe location."

When she didn't reply, I glanced at her and tried to catch my breath from the adrenaline rush. She glowered right back, her kissable lips thin in a firm line as she stared me down.

"I'm taking you to a safe location."

She narrowed her eyes more, not speaking.

"Do you hear me?"

"How could I not when you're shouting at me?" she sassed back.

"What the fuck is your problem?" I volleyed my attention again, looking back to see if any cars were coming and forward again as I checked the route ahead. "I—"

Don't. Don't lash out. Keep your cool. She's shocked and traumatized and... I whooshed out a long breath. "I'm taking you to a safe location."

"Of your choice? *You'll* decide that?"

"Yes!" I again shot her a side-eye, trying my hardest not to be annoyed at her attitude after I'd literally followed those Ilyins to save her.

"Then how are you not kidnapping me?"

"I'm not—"

"Because I am sick of being taken!" She screamed it, fisting her hands as she snarled at me. "I am sick and tired of being taken and controlled."

I licked my lips and forced a dry swallow, minding my temper. She was venting, raging and releasing all that pent-up fear. I recognized that it was happening, and I schooled myself not to react, not to reply in kind with anger and frustration.

"I'm only taking you to a safe location," I repeated.

She didn't speak up. Seething as she turned, giving me her shoulder, she crossed her arms and stared at the window.

"I'm taking you to a safe location," I said once more, just to drive in that reassurance. I felt obligated to treat her like a feral, cornered, and scared animal. "Were you shot?"

No reply.

"Are you seriously injured?"

Again, no reply or reaction.

"Are you—"

She shifted, turning away from me even more, and I clamped my lips shut tight in frustration. She wasn't going to tell me shit. I got it. But she would. There wasn't a chance in hell I was letting her out of my sight now that I had her.

The further I drove, the more I mapped out a rash plan. Lev and Eva would demand that I bring her to the Baranov mansion, but I didn't think that would be the best course of action until I had all my answers. Until this enigmatic woman could explain what was going on, I would keep her where I could control her safety and security.

Looks like the Ilyins really did intend to hold her until they could force her into marriage. Since that day I heard Igor Petrov and Geoff Ilyin talking, when Geoff claimed that they'd had Sonya taken for a future arranged marriage to their benefit, I'd dismissed it as his making up lies to sound impressive. I hadn't wanted to be convinced that they'd actually done that, that the Sonya I'd met and desired could be the woman they were using like that.

But now that I'd found her in the Ilyins' custody, abused and beaten, it seemed that they hadn't been bluffing. They really had taken Sonya. Eva was wrong that her sister had run away.

Yet, there were still too many unknowns I wanted cleared up.

Letting Sonya stew seemed smartest while I tried to figure out how to get her to talk. But the next time I glanced at her, I found her fast asleep. Dark circles lined under her closed eyes, and I sighed at the sight of her at peace. If not at peace, then relaxed to the point where she could rest.

Making up my mind to give her a chance to rest as much as she could in the hopes that she'd open up to me when she wasn't scared or threatened, I drove to one of the remote cabins I owned upstate. While I drove in a different direction from the small town where I'd first encountered her and taken her virginity, I counted on the distance between my place and the city to be an advantage.

She slept the whole way there, and when I parked in front of the small cabin, she still didn't stir.

What happened to you? I furrowed my brow as I opened her door then brought her inside. Carrying her didn't rouse her, and I tried to imagine what had caused her to be this exhausted.

Once I got her inside and secured the cabin, I checked that we had food and essentials for a few days. A glance at my phone showed no reception, but that didn't surprise me. The reception was always terrible out here, and I hoped I wouldn't need to make an emergency call.

I laid her on the only bed here, then tried to check her over for any injuries. It didn't seem like she'd hit her head on the ground, but redness and swollen spots showed from those fuckers hitting her. Nothing seemed too serious, though, from what I could tell. When I lifted her shirt to check her stomach, she snapped to and bolted upright.

"Let me—"

She jack-knifed, sitting up so quickly and bringing her hand forward.

I caught her hand, deflecting her hit. "Easy."

"No! Don't tell me to be easy." She scanned the room, frantic to get off the bed. "I won't be kidnapped again."

I held her back, not letting her scurry away. "I said *easy*," I told her in my most commanding voice.

"Are you kidnapping me?" she asked, sounding like a panicked, broken record.

I frowned at her, not wanting to commit to a yes or no. The answer I gave her would dictate how hard she'd want to fight me off. Deep in my heart, I tried not to let that fantasy entertain me. Because kidnapping—or keeping—Sonya didn't sound so bad. After only seeing her twice before, I was well aware of the spell she'd cast on me.

It wouldn't be a hardship on my part to keep her.

"I'm trying to help you," I said instead.

She didn't lose the furious scowl or intense stare that hinted at zero trust or faith in me.

"I am going to keep you safe, Sonya, while you explain what the fuck is going on."

She pressed her lips tighter together, stubborn to stay silent.

"I need answers."

She tipped her chin up and narrowed her eyes more.

"Dammit, Sonya, talk to me!"

"No." She licked her lips before shutting them tight again. "I'm not telling you anything."

"You owe me some answers."

She gaped at me. "I don't owe you—"

I lowered my hand to tug up her shirt, exposing that small bump. I hadn't noticed it at the strip club, and I was shocked how I hadn't. Sure, I'd been distracted by desire, wanting her, but…

"Is this my child?" I stared her down, daring her to lie. "Is this my baby in there that fucker wanted to hurt?" I couldn't help the enraged growl in my tone. Flashbacks of her being held and attacked infuriated me all over again. But to aim for harming my child, too?

Sniffling once, she nodded. "From…" Her throat flexed with a swallow. "From when I saw you at the bar and…"

"It's mine?" I had to ask again. I had to hear her confirm it again to erase the doubt. I hadn't wanted to get my hopes up high.

She nodded a little more firmly. "I gave my virginity to you that night. And no one else has touched me since."

I was going to be a father. She'd confirmed it, and I didn't detect a lie in her quiet, sheepish admission.

I would have a child.

Me—I would have a son or daughter to raise and care for.

I'd been loosely wishing I could slow down and settle with someone. Turning forty had been on my mind a lot lately. But to actually already have a child on the way…

I exhaled a long breath as I stared at her.

"I didn't let them. I couldn't let them hurt my baby."

I set my hand on her stomach, so moved and overwhelmed with indescribable emotions that I could barely breathe past it all. Awe. Shock. Wonder. Excitement. Utter surprise.

"*Our* baby."

I admired the contrast of my darker, tanned skin with my fingers over her pale belly. Feeling this soulful and heartfelt connection to Sonya seemed like a mystery I'd never solve, but knowing she really would be the mother of my child? I couldn't get over it. I couldn't accept the miracle of it and let it sink in.

"Our baby," I repeated. "One you didn't bother to mention when I spotted you running through that strip club."

"Oh, you mean when you pretended not to recognize me in that little room? You want answers from me, but I demand them from *you*, whoever the hell you are."

"I'm the father of this baby," I said, slanting over her on the bed. I couldn't help the smile on my face. This was serious business, but just saying it out loud got to me.

I would be a *father*.

"Yeah, but..." She frowned slightly, reclining as I advanced over her on the bed. "But I don't even know who you are or why or how—"

I closed the distance between us, lunging in for a kiss. It was swift, hard, unforgiving and full of all the awe and marvel of her and the fact that we had a baby to look forward to.

"I'm the father of this baby," I reminded her as I stroked up her stomach, rewarded with the gasp of surprise she gave at my touch.

Hovering over her more, I kissed her again. "I'm the man who took your virginity."

She licked her lips after that kiss. "But why did you pretend not to know me at that club?"

I tugged her shirt off. "You faked it too."

"I didn't fake *it*."

I grinned, mesmerized by how this immediate, potent desire rendered her helpless to needing my touch too. Lust warmed up her gaze, and she moaned when I kissed her again. "You faked not knowing who I was."

"Only because you did first."

As I kissed her again and again, giving up on seducing some answers out of her, I slowly got our clothes off until this burning need to have her again was all that I could think of. "You've been in my life as nothing but a mystery, Sonya." I urged her to part her legs for me, and she did.

"I barely *know* you."

I lined up my dick and nudged inside, robbing her of speech. Low, sexy moans left her lips now.

"There are too many questions about you, too many things that don't add up yet." I almost closed my eyes at how good it felt to thrust all the way into her. "I was surprised to see you, and it seemed easier to focus on this" —I pulled out and slid back in quickly— "instead of interrogating you."

"Oh, fuck." She hugged me close, already writhing slightly. "Yeah. I… Yeah. I want to focus on your doing this too."

Mindful of where she had to have been injured and hit, I fucked her. Steadily. Slowly. Thoroughly, only letting her get close to coming when she seemed ready to explode. A hard, fast quickie could be just as hot as a slow, lazy fuck.

"But after," I promised her, panting as I strained to breathe through the exertion of holding myself back, "after, we're going to talk."

She shook her head, but I couldn't tell if she was arguing or just thrashing to come. Her pussy gloved me so tightly that I wouldn't last. She felt too good. She tempted me to let go and embrace this sense of belonging that knitted us together so close.

We will. As soon as I could please her and watch her face as she hit her orgasm, we would talk.

"I'm not letting you go," I mumbled between short, harsh breaths as I resisted the urge to come. I had to wait for her, and blessedly, she came.

Crying out, she clenched around me and rode out the pleasure. Her face contorted into that intense wince of bliss. Her legs trembled as she kept them slung around me. And her inner walls clenched and squeezed, triggering me to come so hard that I wanted to bellow and roar. I shot my hot cum deep inside her. I let the tingles of that electric thrill chase down my spine. And I relished the slick fit of her pussy milking me until I was dry.

Mine.

I rolled over, keeping her close. Our cum stuck to our legs as she moved onto her side with me, and I couldn't help but lower my gaze toward her stomach.

Ours.

I kissed her once more.

You're mine. I placed my hand over her stomach. *And it's my turn to protect what is ours.*

17

SONYA

I closed my eyes as I relaxed against Ben's warm chest. This hard wall of muscles was already so familiar, which seemed bizarre with how crazy my life was lately.

I'd told myself now wasn't the time for sex or distractions. I was devoted, stubbornly devoted to the goal of getting back to whatever remained of my family. But I hadn't yet accepted that I now had another family of my own making, my baby in my belly and his or her father lying with me.

His cum was drying on my thigh because I'd caved once again.

"Is Ben even your name?"

A grunt was his reply. Or maybe that was a laugh. It seemed that he thought I was asleep and hadn't been expecting me to talk.

"Yes. My name is Ben."

I shifted so I could face his rugged, bearded face. Peering at him, I tried to understand how my body and heart could recognize him as someone who could help me, who could care to protect me and pleasure me, but I had no clue who the hell he actually was.

He opened his mouth to speak, breaking under the pressure of the silence first, but I covered his lips with my fingers.

"Are you kidnapping me?"

He frowned. "After what we just did, you still have to ask?" He used the sheet to wipe the cum on my leg.

"I have been captive too long, and I refuse to be in that position again."

He opened his mouth to speak and I covered it again. But this time, he dodged my hand and urged me to get up with him.

"You know more about me than I do you. I know nothing, Ben. Not who you are. How we ran into each other again. How you knew to save me and—" I drew in a quick breath, not ready to ramble this quickly.

Holding his hand, I admired his ass as he led me from the bed and to a small bathroom.

"I have been told nothing for eleven years. I haven't had access to anyone. No phone, no TV, no devices to keep me aware of anything happening outside the room I was kept in. So I am in the dark more than you could be."

He started a shower, watching me as he turned the faucets. Then without a word, he got into the steamy stall with me.

"My name is Ben. Ben Warner."

I narrowed my eyes at him as he hugged me close. Water streamed over us, soothing me. "Warner? I heard you curse in Russian at that strip club."

"I lived in Russia until my mother brought me to the States. I'm a contractor."

"An assassin?" I guessed. No man could shoot that many dead with ease like he did without experience in murdering before.

He nodded. "I'm an independent contractor." He shrugged, then slicked the water off his hair. "Until now. Maybe."

That needed more explanation, but later. "How did you find me?"

"The first time, I didn't. You did. You found me at that bar. I saw you come in and scan the crowd. You came to me."

I nodded.

"Why?"

"I told you. I wanted to lose my virginity. You were a stranger who caught my eye, and that was that."

He peered at me for a long moment, seeming to search for his next words. We were both so guarded, tiptoeing around each other verbally in what had to be the oddest connection. Steam swirled around us, calming me, but I remained tense and eager to hear what he'd say next.

"I was in that area to kill an Ilyin guard. And then there you were."

"Go on."

He arched a brow, not wanting to divulge too much and still expecting me to fill in some blanks. "Go on to what? You took off and I never saw you until that night at the strip club."

"Why were you there?"

He began washing my hair gently, worrying me that he wouldn't reply.

"I was following a target," he said as I shivered under the caress of his fingers on my scalp. "I've done hits for all the Mafia families as an independent. I'd killed for the Cartels and gangs too. But lately, I've been on jobs near you."

I narrowed my eyes. "So I'm supposed to believe we just happened to be near each other? It was a coincidence to run into you there?"

"Yes." He ceased the heavenly massage on my head that I wanted to moan at. Rinsing my hair felt just as good.

"And no. I heard about you in passing. When I heard your name, I wondered if those people could be talking about you, the virgin I couldn't stop thinking about. The sexy woman I wanted again."

He kissed me deeply then stepped back to grab a loofah and soap to wash me.

I refused to melt under his sweet words and tender touches. I had to stay focused before I'd let myself relax. "Who was talking about me?"

"Igor Petrov and Geoff Ilyin. They were discussing how they wanted to end the Baranov family and power."

I growled. Our rivals would plot the Baranov demise. I didn't doubt that for a second. "What do you mean, they *want* to end us?" It felt good not to have to pretend I wasn't a Mafia princess around him, that I wasn't Sonya Baranov. "We *are* done."

He furrowed his brow at me, washing me.

"My father was killed—"

"Wait. How did you hear about Boris dying? That happened recently. If you weren't told anything in years—"

"I overheard the guards outside my room speaking. That's why I had to escape. I can't let my family be diminished to nothing. I can't let Eva be vulnerable and alone without anyone to protect her. My mother was killed years ago. Uncle Oleg has been gone for so long too. It's just me trying to get back to Eva and…"

He'd started to slowly shake his head in the middle of my ramble.

"What?" I asked, my heart racing. Deep down in my gut, I just knew he was about to say something that would shock me and rattle me further than I already was. The moment had come. I'd *finally* get some intel about what remained of the Baranov legacy.

"That's not true."

"What isn't?" I asked, daring to hope.

"Boris died of a stroke, they think. A natural cause. He was not killed by another."

"Can anyone confirm that?" I asked. My father was a useless alcoholic, but I assumed he'd been forced to clean up after Uncle Oleg died. Wanting the boss of the Baranovs dead would be a prime goal for the Petrovs or Ilyins, or any other syndicated crime organization.

"No one knows what happened to your mother, but—"

It was my turn to shake my head. I did so sadly, lowering my gaze. "*I know. I can confirm that she was killed. She was taken with me, raped and abused countless times. When they wanted to—*" I swallowed, forcing my throat to work past the clogged emotions threatening to choke me. "They wanted to rape me, even though I had to remain pure. Not to take my virginity but…"

He cursed, pulling me into a hug and keeping me in a crushing hug. The injuries from the beating ached more under his tight hold, but it also secured me. I closed my eyes and let the familiarity of his hard body soothe my soul.

"They wanted to rape me there. To fuck my ass. She fought them, begging them not to hurt me at all. So they raped her in my place, to teach her a lesson. To teach me a lesson. While they did it, she took a knife off them and got it to me, and I attacked."

His big hand roved up and down my back, comforting me. Years of therapy would help me get over this trauma, but right now, like this, I felt freer to open up to this man.

"I nearly killed one. But they didn't retaliate and hurt me. They forced me to watch them kill her. And defile her more. It got the attention of the guards' supervisor, though, and because he knew how much I was worth, he prevented anyone from trying to rape me in any way after that. But I saw with my own eyes the moment my mother died, trying to protect me."

We stood, steaming in the shower with the silence surrounding us. If only the water could rinse away my memories of that fateful day years ago.

"You said that wasn't true," I reminded him once I felt calmer and steadier to resume our conversation again. "That Eva isn't alone."

"Because she's not. Oleg lives."

I jerked up to face him. "He does?"

He furrowed his brow again. "Why would you think otherwise?"

"Again, because I heard the guards talking. Maybe I didn't get the whole story, but they seemed to make it sound like Oleg had been killed."

"No. He's alive. Well, yeah, he's alive."

"Huh?" His doubt about stating that bothered me. "Is he or isn't he?"

"Yes, he's alive, but he's suffered a heart attack recently. He's been stressed looking for *you*, apparently. There have been mixed feelings within your family about whether you lived, had been killed, or had run away when you disappeared, but—"

"*Run away?*" I gaped at him. "I would never. I have never lost hope that I could return to my family."

He kissed my brow. "Lev hired me to kill someone, but when I mentioned to him what I'd heard about you and the plans to bring down the Baranov name, he said he would hire me to find you *after* I finished my hit. Oleg had been searching for you for years to no avail, and they have not given up hope, even while Oleg is unable to lead."

I blinked, stunned and overwhelmed by all this news. I would need a lot more time to digest all of this, but I concentrated on this new hope and joy blooming in my chest.

"Uncle Oleg is alive," I repeated.

It was surreal to be able to think that, let alone say it. Adjusting all the visions I had of my uncle being gone would take time, but I wanted to welcome this shocking twist.

Alive! Not dead!

"He is alive. He's currently in a coma and under constant care, but his prognosis is positive."

"Eva isn't alone and unprotected." I gazed up at Ben, thrilled. I didn't try to hide the smile on my lips. For once in a long, long time, I felt free to express happiness.

"No. She never was while you were gone. Oleg was there. So was Boris, even if he did nothing. And as of a month ago, she has Lev as a husband, too."

My jaw would hit the floor at this rate. "Eva married *Lev*? The Baranov soldier Uncle Oleg took in?"

He nodded. "He's more or less Oleg's right-hand man now."

"Eva *wanted* to marry him?"

He chuckled, a rich, deep sound I wanted to hear more often.

"Yes. They chose each other in marriage. Oleg asked him to be her bodyguard while she attended college and—"

"Wait." I grinned wider. "Eva went to college?" How bold of her.

"Yeah. And after that experience, um, they… wanted to be together."

I sighed happily. "My father didn't try to use her in an arranged marriage?"

"No. Boris wouldn't have had any say in that decision. Oleg has called the shots, and it seemed he had no interest in an arranged marriage to gain or hold on to an alliance or power. I once heard Rurik say Oleg preferred to orchestrate alliances and power on his own, not through a marriage."

That actually did sound like my uncle. He was always so stubborn and autocratic like that.

"I saw Lev and Eva at their wedding. I wasn't a guest, but I wanted to watch them all and get a better feeling for the members at the top of the Baranov family. So I snuck in."

I couldn't help a laugh. "You spied on them at their wedding?"

He almost smiled. Maybe it was too grave of a thing to joke about because he sobered quickly. "I did. In my position, I need all the intel and facts that I can get before I act on a job or contract. I prefer to be knowledgeable and form my own opinions and make my independent choices about whom I work with or for. I've never formed a loyalty to any one group, not since I left the military. It's why I've been determined to find you myself—before I handled the hit that Lev wants done."

"And Eva is happy?"

He nodded. "For all intents and purposes, and as far as I could witness, she looks like a happy bride, a willing bride, and a woman very much in love with her new husband."

I sighed again, unable to stop letting out all the pent-up worries that my sister could be alone and targeted. Ben noticed my relief, hugging me close, and we finished rinsing off.

"The mood changed pretty quickly when Boris fell over, but—"

I gasped. "He died *at* her wedding?"

He nodded. "He did. She and Lev didn't seem surprised, but they've taken it in stride."

Finished with the shower, we got out. Ben steadied me as I stepped onto the mat, then he dried us both off, still speaking. "Lev respected that Oleg wouldn't stop looking for you. Like I said, he planned to hire me to track you down, but I couldn't ignore this hunch that you were closer than anyone realized."

I shook my head, watching him and wondering how I'd ever lucked out to have him in my life. "Not until recently, when I escaped."

"I wanted to find you because I couldn't forget you, Sonya. It wasn't just a duty. It wasn't just a job. Every time I thought about you, I missed you. I can't explain it. I won't try to justify it. It's just what I felt. But when Lev hinted at hiring me to locate you, it was all I could think about."

Taking the initiative, I leaned up to kiss him, slow and soft. I hoped that I showed how much his admission mattered to me.

"I never forgot you either."

He lowered his hand to my stomach, chuckling lightly again. "Well, I doubt you could. Because I left a little something behind for you to remember me by."

"True." Dazed and so relieved with this good news about my family, I felt dragged down and even more tired than before. The high of relief, the bliss of coming, and then the heat of the shower. All this promising news. I was on cloud nine, floating and hopeful, and it wore me out.

When I yawned again, he smiled and guided me back toward the bed. First, he flung the messed up top sheet off, then he urged me to get under the covers. "Tired?"

"All the time."

"Relax, Sonya. You're safe here."

I would never tire of his saying that. Because I believed it.

For the first time in years, I felt how secure I could be.

"We still have a lot to discuss," he added as he dimmed the lights, waiting for me to settle in.

I nodded, already closing my eyes. "Yeah. We do."

The baby. Us. My family. My captivity. His hit. The future.

I smiled wide as he joined me, spooning me. Everything was changing so fast. But I relished the idea that I could actually look forward to the future for once—that I had a future waiting for me that didn't include being forced into a marriage I didn't want.

18

BEN

Sonya rested on and off for two days. She didn't sleep the entire time, but she was sluggish and safe to stay in bed after all that running and hiding. I'd never had a woman in my life for more than one night or one experience, so she was already an outlier. I'd also never pampered a woman, and it was becoming addicting.

I couldn't begin to imagine how difficult it had been for her to be on the run while pregnant. I didn't want to stop and consider how horrible it was to worry about her family after all the trauma she'd faced, either.

Kidnapped. Almost raped. Forced to witness her mother's death. Withheld from the rest of the world and driven anxious with not knowing what had happened to her sister. Attacked.

I ground my teeth and tamped down the residual anger at the flashbacks I still suffered of her trying to protect her baby from being harmed. *Our* baby. We had yet to speak about the fact that we were having a kid together, but we would. I wouldn't rush it. It'd be better to let her have her head on straight again and not be completely stuck in survival mode to discuss our child.

Mafia families were a different breed. Members of these kinds of families were stronger and tougher, born to endure hardships like no other. For a short time, I had been involved in a different Mafia group in Russia. My mother was a US citizen who'd given birth to me in LA, but she'd been taken back to Russia, where my father was, as a Bratva wife. When he was killed, my mother and I were rejected and sent away. Still, that limited time in a Bratva had given me a crash course on how thick my skin would need to be, how dangerous my life would inherently always be just because I was "one of them".

And Sonya was no weakling. She was the bravest woman I'd ever met to survive what she had. Yet, her body and soul needed to rest. She had to lower her guard a little more and see me as a figure of help she could rely on for more than the offer of a warm bed and protection.

Her sleeping in and being lazy here with me at my remote cabin was probably the first time in years that she'd been able to lower her guard at all. And when she woke up and had meals with me, I enjoyed the gift of providing for her. Feeding her, bathing her, helping her get comfortable, I took care of her, and it was the first time in my life that I felt certain I was being what I was meant to be.

A lover. A partner. A father-to-be. Seeing to her comfort satisfied me, and I knew I was a goner. Just like that, making Sonya happy was my vocation in life.

It helped that she gradually opened up to me too, providing more information, but she was still cautious. I saw it in her eyes. When she gazed at me with desire, it was too easy for me to cave and give in to take her, but I held myself back. We hadn't fucked since that first time she woke up here. And I wouldn't let sex be a distraction from our connecting like partners.

"They took me at the same time they took my mother and kept us together at first," she said over a lunch of tomato soup and grilled cheese. I was glad I kept this cabin stocked with non-perishables. A short trip into town while she napped got the fresh essentials, too.

This was the mother of my child. Of course, she needed good nourishment.

"Was it always the Ilyins?" I asked.

She nodded. "Yes. No middle men. They took us and kept us together. No one but the same few men handled our captivity. The crews changed over the years, obviously. Eleven years is a long shift for a soldier, but even still, they were consistent. Except for the few who got too greedy. Like I said, they killed my mother."

"No one ever knew," I replied.

She nodded sadly. "I bet not."

That had to be the hardest part of it all, the lack of knowing what had happened. Eva seemed a little bitter, resentful with her assumption that her mother ran and took Sonya with her, abandoning Eva at home. And Oleg was vested in learning what happened. He never stopped or gave up on the case. It sounded like he'd recently had Vik go to Moscow to follow a lead about Sonya that turned out to be a dead end.

Sonya had to have suffered all that time, worried about her family.

So why hasn't she just gone back already? I wanted to be careful about how I posed that question. For a short while, I'd been playing with the *what-if* that she could've run away and was acting like a spy against her family. Of course, it was nothing like that. I knew that now. But I couldn't stop being curious about why she didn't run right to her home.

Lev called me earlier, asking what was taking so long about the hit placed on O'Malley. It would've been better to come clean and just tell him that I'd found Sonya and was taking care of her, but that might not have ended well. He could've insisted I bring her to the house, and I didn't want to until she and I talked about this baby, until I had all the information I felt I needed.

However, Lev had given the update no one wanted to hear. Oleg wasn't doing so well. His vitals were mostly stable, but they were all getting more concerned about the length and depth of his coma after his heart attack.

Time wasn't on my side. If Sonya wanted to get back to her family, I had to facilitate that sooner rather than later. Which meant I needed answers now.

"How come you snuck out to lose your virginity?" I asked, hoping she wouldn't get quiet and closed-lipped again.

She almost smiled, glancing at me as if she were proud I'd taken her virginity. Just as quickly, she scowled. "I heard them saying I would be taken to my fiancé soon. And I refused to let them take that one last thing from me. They'd taken my mother, they'd taken *me*, they'd taken my freedom, and I didn't want them to have control over who took my virginity as well. It was the last thing I had, and I wanted to reclaim control, even just for a moment."

"You wanted to stick it to them, huh?"

She nodded, lowering her hand to rest it on her belly. "And I don't regret it."

"You don't regret that it was me? Or that you got knocked up?"

Now she really smiled. "Both. I'm glad it was you. And despite the hell that I am bringing this baby into, I can't wait to be a mother. It's a dream I never could've imagined being able to have. I feared being married off to someone I didn't want, then bred and expected to let them take my children to raise as soldiers or future brides."

I couldn't help it. Leaning over, I claimed her lips in a kiss. I kept it soft and gentle, but once she sighed against me, I was relieved I hadn't made a mistake. We hadn't been intimate for the last couple of days—that was my doing. But with this little step of a kiss, I felt so much hope.

"And it's why I escaped when I did. Once more, I overheard the guards talking about transporting me to my fiancé. I knew I was pregnant by then. I'd missed my period three times and I felt my body changing. So I worried not only to be forced into a marriage that I didn't want but also that there would be no way to hide that I wasn't a virgin anymore. I feared they'd take my child, and so I fought hard to run."

I took her hand, glad when she didn't flinch or retreat. Stroking my thumb over her knuckle, I waited for her to continue. "How did you get away?"

"I hid a butter knife under my pillow and waited for the guards to enter my room. I attacked them both, using the knife to kill one. Then, with..." She shook her head, like she couldn't believe it herself. "Then with some kind of mother's instinct to survive and see to my baby's survival, I fought like hell and wounded the second guard so I could take his keys, climb out the window, and drive away. They chased me, but when I crashed, I got out and ran into the woods for hours to lose them. And I did."

"Damn." I picked up her hand to kiss the back of it. "I hate that you had to do that alone."

"I wasn't. I had him or her motivating me." She smiled at her stomach. "And then I found a cabin with a small family in it. Jenny and Kyle Peterson." When she described the young mother who was also a vet, I smiled along with her.

"As soon as I can, I'm paying them back."

Me too. I wouldn't hesitate to show gratitude for the people who'd selflessly saved my woman and child.

"If you took his truck, how come you didn't drive straight to the Baranov home?" I asked.

"The truck died. So I hitchhiked." She worried me with her telling of the woman who tried to rob her. "And I walked. And walked. I had no phone. Nothing. I couldn't call for a ride. When I got into the city, the driver refused to take me there, too afraid because it was a Mafia residence. No driver wanted to drive there, and I suppose that makes sense. The Baranov name holds power still. It invokes fear."

I nodded. "It does. Even with Oleg out at the moment, Lev and the others are making sure nothing happens."

"I knew I needed more information before going home. I wanted to make sure I wasn't entering a dangerous situation, thinking that without any leader, another family could be taking over. I just didn't know. I didn't know anything about what was happening, so I got a room to sleep in and catch my breath before trying to get home. That was how I ended up at Mancy's. I recalled that it was Eva's favorite restaurant, and I just so lucked out seeing her there." She furrowed her brow. "But then when I saw that Petrov woman, I was confused and worried."

"Irina Petrov," I explained. "Soon to be Mrs. Vik Baranov."

Her jaw dropped. *"What?"*

"Irina isn't the enemy, even though her surname was—is—Petrov. She and Vik got together when he was undercover at the college, posing as a professor to investigate what the Petrovs and Ilyins were doing in regard to the drug trade there."

"Vik is going to marry her?"

I nodded. "Yes, and it turns out that Irina has a younger brother who is *your* brother, too."

Her jaw dropped. "What? What do you mean?" She furrowed her brow. "My *mother*? No. That's impossible."

"Boris," I explained. "Boris had an affair with Igor's wife, and Igor pretended the boy, Maxim, was his. He planned to use Maxim as leverage with Oleg one day, having a Baranov offspring under his custody." I held up my hand. "It sounds like a complicated story, and I know Irina, Vik, or even Oleg will be able to explain it to you better."

She blinked. "Wow."

"So Irina is not the enemy."

"Okay, but I didn't know that. I saw her and knew she was a Petrov, and I worried that Eva wasn't safe, maybe not even safe to approach. When I saw them at Mancy's, I was afraid I'd be captured, so I ran. I ran into *you*, precisely, at the strip club next door, and..." She shrugged. "We both know what happened there."

"Yeah. You couldn't resist me."

She smirked. "Nor could you resist me."

I smiled. "Guilty as charged. But why did you run again?"

"Because I didn't know who you were or if you'd be able to help me. At that time, you were still Ben the one-night stand, Ben the stranger who was my baby's daddy. After that, I tried to figure out how to get ahold of someone back at the house, but when I was going to the store to buy bread, I felt so weak and nauseated that I knocked into a shelf. The woman working at the store thought I was shoplifting, and she called the cops."

I sighed. "Let me guess."

She rolled her hand as though to say *go ahead*.

"The cops contacted the Ilyins and they captured you again."

"Yes. And that was where you found me. How did you, though? I know you said Lev was considering hiring you to find me after you did this hit, but...?"

"I was trying to find a lead—for how I could get close to my hit and how to find you. O'Malley was injured at that shootout at the strip club, and I couldn't get close to kill him. But I noticed some Ilyins were hanging around the hospital he was in, so I followed them and overheard them talk about going to help with a woman they'd recaptured. Which was you."

"Clearly, the Ilyins are getting around. They have the cops working for them," she replied.

"Not just the cops, but the next governor. O'Malley will be sworn in soon. I think the Ilyins are one step ahead of Igor Petrov in allying with power."

She was quiet for a moment as she raised her brows. "Is that why Lev wants O'Malley taken out?"

"Yes. O'Malley seems to be favoring one family over the other, and the Ilyins seem to want to be his favorite. And that's also how I first heard your name and wondered if my sexy virgin was someone of more importance. I spied on Igor Petrov and Geoff Ilyin after Boris died because I wanted to know if they'd killed him."

"You really do like being in the know, huh?"

"I have to be. Geoff and Igor made it no secret that they want to end your family. Geoff told Igor that he had it covered. He'd had *you* taken. They took you to save as a forced bride for Eric Benson, who is a congressman waiting to be sworn in. The Benson family has always been involved with certain families, and it seemed that the Ilyins figured they would rule at the top by forcing a Baranov to be married to a Benson. So that once Eric was in office and you were his leverage as his wife…"

"Then he'd be able to attack my family through the connection to me." She narrowed her eyes. "It won't happen." Again, she laid her hand over her stomach, protective without realizing it.

"No, it won't," I agreed. "Benson isn't getting near you."

"And they will not weaken the Baranov legacy. I won't marry him. Eva won't be forced to either." She sat up straight. "I'm devoted to my family, and as soon as I can get back to them, I will ensure that Benson is killed." With her free hand, she slashed through the air. "He won't threaten me again. He won't threaten this baby."

Releasing her hand, I leaned in to frame her face and kiss her. "He's dead," I promised.

She let out a shaky breath at my words, probably seeing them as a vow. And they were. As I helped her onto my lap, she hugged me close. "He's dead, Sonya. No one and nothing will endanger you or our child. I will see to it."

Nodding slightly, she nestled against me. If this wasn't the ultimate demonstration of her trust, her words were.

"Take me home, Ben. I'm ready to see my family and stand with them again."

Consider it done. "All right. Tomorrow."

"I'm ready to be reunited with my family," she added. "Since my other family seems to be right here where I want it." Taking my hand to hold it, she lowered it toward her baby bump.

I didn't want to misinterpret her words, but I was elated at the idea that she could see *me* as someone in her family. That the three of us could be a family within the Baranov legacy.

19

SONYA

Ben drove us back into the city the next day.

It still felt like it was too soon. It seemed like I was venturing into the unknown and embarking on a dangerous mission that could go so wrong. But it wasn't. I was simply coming home.

I'd dreamed of it all those years I was gone. That fiery need to come back to the house I grew up in was never extinguished, but with time, I lost hope. It was inevitable that my hope would falter the longer I was stuck on the Ilyin property, but I hadn't given up.

Now that the time had come and I was being taken directly back there, I was nervous. Tension claimed me, and I struggled with realizing that I could view this trip as something bad, as something negative to brace for.

"What has you so worried over there?" Ben asked calmly. He didn't take his gaze off the road, and his tone was calm and neutral. He wasn't teasing, nor was he demanding.

"You think I'm worried?" I huffed a little laugh.

"I *know* you're worried. I can tell."

I smirked at his profile. "You think you can claim to know me already?"

He dragged his focus off the road and gave me a slow once-over. "I've been learning quickly."

Oh, whoa. That smoldering look heated me right up. I had been alarmed when he didn't try to make a move on me after that shower. It seemed that we were so quick to fall into each other's arms whenever we saw each other, but he didn't reach out for me with desire again.

Three days, he'd been there taking care of me and giving me no pressure to do anything. He let me call the shots of what it would be like to be in that cabin, and all I had wanted to do was sleep and rest. I needed it, and somehow, he anticipated giving me space and time like that.

When he kissed me yesterday, hope bloomed again. My heart felt so full when he reached over to kiss me while we talked. It was proof that he wasn't uninterested. Even with that kiss, he was showing me that he could give me space. That kiss was just a kiss, not a prelude to fucking, and that made it all the sweeter. Tender.

I guess if I'm going to fall head over heels for someone, it'd be a man like him.

Tough, no-nonsense, stern. Yeah, he checked all the boxes I hadn't realized I'd organized.

But this is still not the time for that.

I had to see my family. I needed to know Benson would be killed. I wanted to eliminate any and all threats against me and my baby.

Wait. How—

"Will Oleg wage war against the Ilyins for how they'd taken me and held me captive?"

Never mind wondering how well Ben could think he knew me. I had to focus.

"I would be surprised if he didn't. If, for some reason, he doesn't, then I'll take them out."

I blinked. "All of them?"

He glanced at me, almost deadpan.

Well, he did pick off all the men at that warehouse...

Picturing Ben avenging me and killing my enemies was a nice image to hold on to. Yet, at the same time, I hated the smidgen of doubt. Would he, though? He said he was an independent contractor, and taking out a Mafia family wasn't something an independent would do.

It felt so good to lean on him and trust him, but I worried I was looking at him too naïvely. I couldn't help but imagine him being with me, staying with me and wanting our child. Like a real family. Like Jenny and Kyle with baby Damon.

Stop. I had to chide myself and quit this silliness. I was getting way too ahead of myself with thoughts like that.

First things first. I had to go home and see my uncle and sister again. They deserved to know and see firsthand that I was okay. All my worries about my return faded the more that I reassured myself I wasn't doing this alone. Ben was here, and it didn't look like he'd leave me or betray me.

When he neared the city, he turned in a way that wouldn't lead to the mansion.

"They're not at the house," he explained. "I'll take you there if you want, but in order to see your family, they'll all be at the hospital visiting Oleg. Or on their way to do so."

I nodded. "That makes sense."

At the hospital, I had a fleeting wish that I could be here for any other reason. Like... maybe coming to check on the baby in my belly. I worried about the lack of prenatal care so far, but I had to convince myself that I would soon have access to the medical care I deserved.

Ben snuck me into the hospital with ease. For as tall as he was, it was almost amazing how well he could prevent himself from standing out. Ben blended in like a pro, and I was grateful he was the random stranger I'd found all those months ago. Only him.

"You've done this before, huh?" I asked wryly once we were in the elevator going up to my uncle's floor. "Trespassing and sneaking around."

He smiled and winked, no doubt proud of his stealth and memory of codes at doors. "It comes naturally."

Once we reached the correct floor, he took my hand and guided me out. Making sure that I followed him, he proved again and again how protective he wanted to be over me.

Instead of knocking, he used another code on a panel to unlock a door.

My heart raced. Anticipation built again. The surface of my palm had to be so slick with nervous sweat, but Ben didn't let go once.

I noticed the slight stiffening of his fingers as they tightened around my hand, though, and I knew at once that something was wrong.

None of my family members were in here but one. Uncle Oleg was alive, if pale and unconscious. Seeing him in the flesh after so long of thinking he was dead should've brought happy tears to my eyes. Instead, I narrowed them and braced myself for violence.

Ben urged me to stay back as he ran forward. His target was the man trying to place a pillow over Uncle Oleg's face. He was going to smother him! But Ben was there. Rushing over, he halted the man from ever placing the fabric over Uncle Oleg at all.

While Ben fought the man back, I didn't waste a second going for the other person trying to mess with my uncle. A woman in a nurse's uniform got up from the floor. Dazed and shaking her head, she seemed to be coming to after being knocked over and out. In her hand was a syringe, though, and she wasn't getting through my uncle's skin, not while I was here.

"Stop!" I lunged at her, mindful of not letting her lash out and hit my stomach. Fighting while trying to cover my abdomen wasn't easy, but I did it. We struck out and resisted, facing each other off, and with my experience of self-defense, I got her into a chokehold.

As I fought her, I lost track of Ben in the room, but he was there. Right at my side, he came to take over holding the nurse still.

"What is going on?" I asked, panting from the exertion of the fight. A glance to the side showed the man on the floor. But I checked another look at my uncle again, alarmed that people would be in here to harm him. Where were the guards? Why wasn't he protected?

"He's a Petrov soldier," Ben said, not tearing his serious scowl away from the woman. "He was here to kill Oleg."

Was? I took that to mean Ben had killed the guy already and he wasn't just lying on the floor unconscious.

"Let me go!" the nurse protested as she wriggled and flailed to get free. "I'm just a nurse and, and, and, I'll call security!"

"Why would you be giving him a shot?" Ben demanded. He didn't release her. "If he needs medication, they push it in his IV line."

"This is different," she argued, her eyes frantic and open wide as she searched for a way to get out of his grip.

I swallowed hard, my mouth so dry, as I calmed down from the fight. Too many things were happening here, and I struggled to stay level-headed. "Different how?" I pointed at the man on the floor before she could answer, asking Ben, "Is he dead? And where are the guards?" Lev couldn't have had Oleg here unsupervised.

Ben tipped his head toward the opposite wall. Behind a chair, I saw the legs of two men lying down, shoved out of sight.

"I should've wondered why the guards weren't at the door when we came. They usually have them take a break when the family is visiting, so I assumed that meant they'd be in here." Ben hardened his features at the nurse again. "What the fuck were you doing?"

"I'm a nurse," she protested.

Ben got his gun out and held it up to the underside of her chin. "Tell me."

Tears leaked from her eyes. She trembled with the gun aimed up at her head. "I'm— I—" She sobbed. "I was told to give him a medicine to make him weak. To weaken his heart further, but slowly, so he'd pass away naturally."

"Fuck," I muttered, scowling at her. As I'd expected, people wanted Oleg dead. My uncle had been alive all this time, but it seemed enemies were trying to change that after all. "Who? Who paid you?"

"A man. I don't know who he is, but someone…"

Ben jammed the gun up harder, forcing her to tip her head back. "Try again."

"Someone named Ilyin."

Ben and I shared a glance. A Petrov was in here to smother Oleg. The Ilyins were bribing a nurse to drug him.

Right then, over the sounds of the nurse crying, the Petrov soldier got up. He wasn't dead, but knocked out. Cursing in Russian, he quickly advanced again. "The Ilyins won't get this kill. Igor will claim his death, and the Petrov name will be respected as holding all the power and—"

Ben didn't let him finish. Before the man could come at us or my uncle on the bed, Ben hurried at him to fight once more. He'd dropped his gun in the flurry of action, though, and I didn't waste time lowering to grab it.

"Please. Please, I beg of you, let me go." The nurse flinched when I grabbed her arm, torn between retreating to get Ben's gun or keeping a firm grip on her.

Digging my fingers into the flesh of her forearm, I fought to keep her close. And I did, almost. She played dirty, flinging out her fist to punch my stomach, and I had to arch back to avoid that impact. Once more, we were engaged in a wrestle, with slaps, strikes, and elbows, but in the scuffle, I managed to get the gun off the floor. With the silencer, it made no noise. Aiming once, at her brow, I fired a single shot, planting a bullet right between her eyes.

Heaving hard and hating how out of breath I felt, I leaned over and pressed my hand to my side. If this wasn't a stitch from the exercise of fighting, it was a cramp. Wincing, I breathed through it and waited for the ache to fade. It did, slowly, but I felt so winded.

"Sonya?"

Ben lowered the dead man to the ground. He *was* dead now, with that fatal crack of his neck. Ben's hands slipped away from the man's head, and he didn't bother watching his kill slump to the floor. His gaze was on me, worried and alarmed.

"Are you okay?"

I nodded, cringing at the aches in my side. They weren't too low in my abdomen, so I was hopeful it was just a sore muscle, not something to do with the baby. "They're dead."

"Yeah." He approached, not losing that worried stare. "They're dead. I'll handle the cleanup."

"I'll help—" As I handed him the gun, I had to stop at the tightening of the cramp in my belly. Putting my hand on Oleg's bed, I waited for the pain to recede.

"Sonya." Ben shoved the gun into its holster at his back. He didn't stop there, though. As soon as his hands were free, he collected me in his arms and encouraged me to lean against him. "Sonya, you're bleeding."

Huh?

I looked down at my arms and hands, guessing that the nurse had injured me in our fight. The only blood I could find was lower, on my thighs. The light-gray leggings I wore showed darker spots of crimson near my crotch.

I lifted my face and furrowed my brow at Ben, realizing why he seemed so worried now.

The baby!

20

BEN

"Easy. Just breathe," I coached. Holding on to Sonya, I guided her toward a chair.

Her cringes and winces couldn't be a good sign. Yes, she was strong. But she was also pregnant and had been pushing it a lot. I was no expert at pregnant women, but I was pretty sure they weren't supposed to engage in combat.

"Just a pulled muscle," she protested weakly as she walked with me toward a chair.

"But that's blood." I looked down again at her. "And that woman didn't have anything like a blade."

"I think..." She faltered in her step, closing her eyes as she winced again.

"Too bad," I growled. I was taking charge. This was our baby she was carrying. A new life neither of us had expected but one I would protect. I didn't care what she thought or wanted at this moment. She needed to be checked out. "Hold on to me."

Before she could protest again, I leaned down to pick her up. As strong as she was, both physically and mentally, it seemed that she'd finally reached the point of trusting me and leaning on me. Tucking her face against me, she clung to me as I carried her out of the room.

I paused only long enough to check that the door to Oleg's room closed behind us. As soon as it was shut, I hurried down the hall to the elevator. "Where is the maternity ward?" I asked the first person I spotted in scrubs and wearing a medical ID.

"What? Hey— Are you all—"

"Where is the maternity ward?" I demanded again.

"Fourth. Fourth floor," the young man said before I rushed by.

I carried Sonya into the elevator, and that was where she fidgeted to be set down. "Settle down. I'm making sure you two are okay."

"I know. But the room. Those bodies…"

She wasn't just talking the talk when she said she was devoted to her family. This brilliant, sharp woman worried about Oleg. And she had a point. With Baranov guards down, that Petrov soldier, and the nurse the Ilyins paid off, there was a lot of cause for concern. Any staff member could walk in and freak out. Lev had to be updated.

I didn't want to call him to gain favor in case I wanted to join the family. I only had to follow through with this cleanup for Sonya's sake. Her worry had to be that spotting of blood, not her uncle.

Adjusting my hold on her as we rode down to the fourth floor, I got my phone out and called him.

"What is it?" he answered.

"I came to see Oleg just now and the guards had been taken down. They're inside his room. I also found a Petrov soldier trying to smother him *and* a nurse the Ilyins paid off to drug him until he died so it'd look like a natural death."

All the while I spat out that rushed explanation, he tried to splutter and cut in. "What?" he demanded, incredulous after I stopped to draw in a breath.

I didn't have time to check what he'd heard. "Get to Oleg's room now. It needs to be cleaned up."

"Wait. What? Where— How— Where are you going? Just wait there for my men. Why were you there at all?"

"Get to his room now," I said again, then hung up. I couldn't answer his questions. Not until I knew that Sonya and our baby were okay.

The elevator arrived on the fourth floor and I carried Sonya off. My initial conversation with the first nurse we found wasn't smooth. I was panicky, but I was direct, impatient, and stern that Sonya be seen. Led to a room, I laid her down and stepped back so she could be assessed.

"Help my wife," I said.

Sonya shot me a look, but I ignored it. If she was nervous about her return, then she could "hide" as my wife. Plus, she couldn't give her name just yet. She'd been missing for eleven years, and I didn't want her personal details shared to the point it could cause an issue. Without a driver's license or insurance or money, she'd stand out. She had nothing—except me, and I had faith she'd play along with my spontaneous lie.

Watching over the nurses and the doctor as they assessed Sonya, I stepped further from the bed and worried. It wasn't much blood, but with my limited knowledge about pregnancies, I feared any blood had to be a bad sign. I didn't know what they could be finding, but I wouldn't leave. So far, I had been her only help. She was so independent, running on her own, but now that she had opened up to trust me, I found that I couldn't let anyone else handle her security or comfort.

While I stayed in the background of her room, telling one nurse my personal info for them to admit her here as "my wife", my phone buzzed. And buzzed.

Lev. And Vik. The Baranov men were relentless in wanting answers. They were no doubt rushing here to handle the situation in Oleg's room. Each time my phone buzzed and I glanced at the screen, I caught Sonya watching me, still worried.

Stop it. Focus on yourself. And the baby. I could run interference, and I did. Each time the doctor or nurse commented that Sonya was stable, I could relax and text back Lev that I'd be there soon to help. All while they hooked Sonya up to monitors, then did an ultrasound on the baby, I did my best to pay attention and also relay the Baranovs' concerns.

"Almost four months," the ultrasound technician reported as she moved the gel-covered wand over Sonya's belly. "And measuring just fine."

The fast thumps of a heartbeat filled the air. In that precious moment of time, hearing our child's heart for the first time, Sonya and I looked at each other and smiled.

That's it. That's my son or daughter.

I still couldn't wrap my head around the idea that I would be a father! I'd be in charge of protecting this sweet baby for the rest of his or her life. And I couldn't wait. I'd already started worrying about Sonya while she carried our child. From the bottom of my heart, I knew I would worry about our baby until my last breath.

Was that what it meant to embrace parenthood? It was happening suddenly for me, but I wouldn't fight it. This felt like the sign I had been waiting for, the catalyst to settling down and being a solitary loner. And I welcomed the thrill of it.

Lev called, again and again, and Sonya couldn't act like she didn't notice.

"Go on." She nodded once as they continued to check the baby.

I shook my head.

"Go see and come back," she added, furrowing her brow as if she wondered if I'd listen.

I sighed, hating to be torn away from her.

"But please…" She licked her lips, glancing at the technician.

The young woman smiled politely. "You know what? I need more gel." She held up the gel container as she placed the ultrasound wand aside on the cart she'd wheeled in. She'd guessed that Sonya and I needed to speak privately. "I'll be right back."

As soon as she was gone, Sonya cleared her throat. "Just please don't tell them about me yet. I want to be reunited with them all, but I'm cautious. With two attempts on Oleg's life, everything is chaotic at the moment. I think they're saying the baby is okay and I'm okay, but I'm nervous about spotting and just—" She exhaled a deep whoosh of a breath.

"I hear you." I leaned in to kiss her brow.

"I mean, that's our baby." She smiled, in awe, at the steady heartbeat. "I want to be able to bring him or her into this world safely."

"Me too."

"And I'm just not ready for them to know I'm alive and here and having your baby and—"

I chuckled, kissing her again. "I get it." And I did. It *was* a handful.

"I'm just worried about too many people knowing where I am yet. I want control over my return."

I nodded, handing her my phone. "I agree. And with that Petrov man in his room and that nurse being paid off, I'm not certain this fucking hospital is even that secure anymore. It would be better for you to remain hidden."

"As Mrs. Ben Warner?" She smiled slyly.

"Are you insinuating I'm not the only one between us who's daydreaming about my being more than just a sperm donor?"

She barked out a single incredulous laugh, but the following smile was so bright and sexy. "I can't even think about that right now. I can't look that far into the future yet."

My heart expanded, filling with hope and excitement at the *yet*.

"And my uncle is in a more dangerous state than I am. The doctor doesn't seem worried—about my health or the baby's."

"True, but—"

"Uncle Oleg can't claim the same. Help Lev and the others. I'll be okay here until you're back."

"Oh, I *will* be back. You're never getting rid of me now."

Again, she smiled.

"But I won't be able to relax being away from you. I don't trust this hospital. I won't trust anyone with your safety."

She sobered, losing the grin. "Not until Benson is dead. I will not rest easy until the man that family took me to marry is killed."

"Like I said, consider it done."

"I won't risk our child being taken someday either."

"I won't risk you or our baby at all. Ever." Taking out my phone, I watched her closely and told her the PIN to unlock the screen. "I'll go, but you keep this. If *anything* happens, call Lev. His number is in the contacts. I'll be with him upstairs until I come back here."

She nodded, accepting the device. After she licked her lips, she gazed up at me with a careful smile. "Be safe."

"Always."

I would—because I had her and our baby to come back to.

21

SONYA

"You sure are a lucky woman, Mrs. Warner." The ultrasound technician returned after Ben left the room. While she resumed rubbing the wand over my belly and checking my baby, she gave me that praise and winked.

I blinked, stunned by too many things at one. One, that anyone could consider me lucky. I had yet to get over the lag of being in captivity. I *was* lucky—now. Two, that I was Ben's wife. I guessed that he'd said that to make it easier for me to be registered and receive care. It implied he'd handle my bill. I appreciated that, of course. I also understood he'd blurted that out in the heat of the moment, in the circumstances of getting me seen as soon as possible, without any questions about who I was and why I didn't have an ID or insurance. His calling me his wife obliterated the need to explain that I had recently been missing for eleven years.

But it was the warmth that enveloped me at the idea that stunned me too.

I wanted him to be my man. I wished he could be my husband. In a bittersweet pang of longing, I wanted Ben to be mine like Kyle was for Jenny. Then Ben would want *me* and welcome our baby.

It felt like such a silly thought to cling to, but with him identifying me as his wife, I dared to hope.

"Yeah, he's a catch."

"So attentive," the tech said, smiling as she continued checking the monitor.

And protective, I wanted to add.

With his phone next to me, I had a lifeline to help until he could return. Impressed that he would stand by me even when he had to go tend to the matters in my uncle's room, I tried to wrap my head around the fact that things could be falling into place in my life after so much loss and hell.

For the next hour, I was thoroughly checked out. Blood was drawn. Ultrasounds were performed. A urinalysis was completed. Then another ultrasound. A nurse also took a while to clean up the wounds I'd received in that fight with the "nurse" in my uncle's room. I hadn't felt the slight scrapes when they happened, too keyed up on adrenaline in the fight to notice, but now that I was being checked out, I realized my skin stung for a reason in those spots.

The doctors came in and out, checking me alongside the technicians, and soon enough, I lost track of who was who and which one specialized in what.

When they asked me for my obstetrics contact, I admitted I didn't have one as I'd only recently learned that I was pregnant. My baby bump was still small, and with how slender I'd always been, it wasn't overly noticeable that I was carrying a baby at all.

I couldn't tell if they believed my lie about not realizing I was pregnant until a couple of weeks ago, but they didn't comment otherwise.

That spared me from having to explain why I didn't already have a doctor for my pregnancy.

"You rest, and we'll get more results in on those labs," the doctor said.

I dared to close my eyes, so exhausted from the stress of the day. I couldn't actually sleep, not with my mind running a mile a minute with questions about Uncle Oleg. I couldn't relax fully with the awe of being able to see him again, even if he had been unconscious. Not to mention my heart, still so full and healing with this concept of letting love in, of letting Ben in and trusting that it wouldn't be a mistake.

Before I could get closer to dozing off, he returned. I had no clue how long he might have been standing there at the door, watching me, but the soft and tender smile on his face soothed my soul.

"Were you watching me sleep?" I teased.

"Were you sleeping?" he teased back.

I shrugged, yawning. "I was close to it."

"Do you want me to go and—"

"No!" I patted the bed and urged him to sit with me.

He joined me, shifting until he could drape his arm around my shoulders. I didn't know how we could fit together so well. It was like he had been made just for me, snug and secure against each other like this.

"How is it going upstairs?"

"Lev and Vik are there, and…" He lifted his face from gazing at me and brushing my hair back from my face. As the doctor returned, he got a more serious expression instead.

"Baby Warner is completely healthy," she announced with an easy smile. "So is Mom."

I sighed, letting all the relief seep through me.

"Spotting can always be scary at first, but it's not always a bad sign."

For the next several minutes, she went over all the information. All the bloodwork results, the ultrasound, everything. With a loose and general instruction to rest and listen to my body during the pregnancy, she gave me—us—a good bill of health.

"Now if you do spot again or have concerns, don't hesitate to check with your doctor." She held out a flyer. "You can find many options for obstetric physicians here."

"Thank you," I told her. Ben thanked her as well, but he waited until she walked out of the room to frame my face and kiss me hard.

"Thank fuck you're okay," he whispered as he stared into my eyes.

I drowned in the affectionate gaze. "And the baby."

"Of course."

I narrowed my eyes. "You didn't look to see whether it was a boy or a girl, did you?"

He chuckled. "Tempted, but no."

"Would you rather have a boy over a girl?"

"I would rather have a healthy baby. That's it."

I licked my lips, realizing we were doing this. We were talking about the fact that we'd have a baby now. It would no longer be an elephant in the room.

"Have you thought about fathering a child?" I asked, hating how nervous I felt to say that. "I can't imagine many independent contract killers who hunt down Mafia men are wild about being tied down with a baby."

"I am. Or I am now." He let out a long but contented exhale, watching my face as he smiled softly. "I'll be forty this year, and I can't deny it's been making me think about settling down. I wouldn't be tied down like it's a burden. I've been gradually wondering how and when I could slow down and start a family. And now…" He picked up my hand and held it as he lowered his gaze to it.

"And now you have one."

"Do I?" he asked, making eye contact again.

"Are you asking me if you're the father of this baby?" I accused, narrowing my eyes.

He chuckled, that delicious, deep sound I was coming to love. "No. I'm asking if I have a family with you. If we're in this together."

"How can you ask that?"

"I can ask that because I need to know." He leaned in to kiss me soundly. "I need to know if you really want to be mine." Another drugging kiss. "If you want to be with me and raise this baby together." Once more, he laid his hot lips on mine, kissing me until I moaned with need. Damn, was he potent.

When he reared back, staring at me, I nodded. "Yeah, I want that, too. I kind of assumed you were interested in… something with me when we kept having sex."

"It's not just sex I want with you," he murmured.

"But I couldn't tell if you wanted me, or what you wanted."

"I want to kill Eric for you. I want to raise our child together. I'll kill O'Malley so he's not a threat. I'll kill the Petrovs and Ilyins. Any rival who threatens you. I want no threats coming from any direction when I'm focusing on my family." A goofy grin lifted his lips. "*My* family. It feels so right to say that. I'm done with the solo, nomadic hitman life, Sonya. I want you. I want our family."

This time, I was the one who leaned in to kiss him deeply. He grunted and held me close, encouraging me to practically climb onto his lap.

Only the nurse coming into the room to discharge me prevented us from getting carried away with lust and need.

As soon as Ben handled the payment and billing details, everything sent to him, we walked out of the room with the peace of mind that nothing was wrong with our baby. Now that I had ultrasound pictures, I felt like it was so much more real. It was stupid to think that. Of course, the baby was real. But seeing him or her in a black-and-white image was different. A pregnancy milestone, I supposed.

"Are you ready to go see Oleg now?" he asked in the elevator. He'd closed the doors but hesitated before tapping a button for a floor. "You didn't really have a chance to see him before."

I nodded. "Is everyone else still up there in his room?"

"Lev will be. Vik too. I bet the women will still be there as well." He tapped the button for Oleg's floor. "Eva is at home, but Irina and Kelly were there when I stopped in there earlier."

"And you didn't tell them I was back?"

"No. I gave you my word, Sonya, and you can always trust in that."

I think I'm already in love with you. I smiled instead of sharing such a declaration. It seemed surreal to fall in love this quickly. Things were moving so rapidly between us, but in life-or-death circumstances, that wasn't too surprising.

We walked toward my uncle's room for the second time. Two Baranov guards stood at the door, narrowing their eyes at us as we approached.

Ben nodded at them.

"Warner," one greeted dryly.

"Lev said no more visitors," the other guard said.

"You're going to tell me I can't see my uncle?" I challenged.

It took them a moment, but they both reacted by dropping their jaws.

"Sonya?" one asked, eyes wide with shock.

I nodded. "If you'll excuse me, I've been waiting eleven years for this moment."

Ben held my hand as he opened the door, leaving the stunned guards outside.

I held my breath slightly, apprehensive about what I'd face in this room this time.

No guard was attempting to smother my uncle. No nurse was on her way to inject something into his body. And no corpses lay on the floor. The cleanup had been done.

Lev spun, furrowing his brow at me. Vik faced us too.

"Holy shit." Vik coughed out an incredulous laugh.

"*Sonya?*" Lev asked, glancing at Ben.

I nodded. "Yes, it's me."

Lev scowled at Ben. "You piece of shit. How many damn secrets are you going to keep from me? From this family?" He gestured at us holding hands. "What's going on?"

"Will it appease you to know that I asked him to keep it a secret for a little bit?" I asked.

Lev turned his stunned expression back to me as he walked closer. "Not really. But you're *here*. You're alive after all."

I laughed at his blunt tone, detecting the joy in it too. We hugged, and Vik wasn't far behind. In a blur of smiles, hugs, and more confused expressions, we embraced each other in this initial return.

Irina was introduced properly. As was Kelly, who was Rurik's wife.

Ben didn't leave my side, and I was proud when Lev and Vik snapped at him and said he had a lot of explaining to do.

"Sonya can explain on her terms," Ben said. "She should be in control of her return."

Okay, that settled it. I was *so* in love with this rugged man. The idea of his letting me call the shots was a huge thing to me.

"Eva won't believe it. She'll—" Lev laughed once. "My God. She will be stunned."

"I can't wait to see her. I've worried about her all the time that I had been gone."

"Just as I've worried about you."

We all stopped, going still at that remark. It hadn't come from anyone standing in the room, but from the bed.

In unison, we faced Uncle Oleg. He was lying in the bed, fully alert as he gazed at me.

He was awake!

"I've worried about you every day you were gone, Sonya." A tear traveled down his cheek.

I choked on a sob, rushing to hug him.

22

BEN

We all stood back as Sonya hugged Oleg. No one would dare to interrupt their reunion, one I doubted either thought they could have.

One second, he was unconscious, and now, he was awake, alert and speaking. The old man didn't seem weak or worn down from being sedated and then slowly coming back to health after his heart attack.

After the team of doctors came into the room at Lev's request, they confirmed the drugs that one nurse had been giving him were what held Oleg back from waking.

"I assure you, Mr. Kvashnin, that we will find that employee and hold her accountable," the head doctor said.

No, you won't.

I helped Rurik drag her dead body out so he could dispose of it. No one would find her, but I imagined this doctor was extra worried about having the Baranov family upset with him or the hospital. Having the Baranovs displeased with their service was a grave mistake they wanted to avoid.

After I left Sonya to be checked out in the maternity ward downstairs, I came back up here and told Lev what I'd found. I handed over the syringe the nurse had, too, and that was what the doctors were given with the expectation that they'd check over Oleg.

All the medical staff members promised that Oleg was stable and wouldn't be permanently harmed by the sedatives that nurse had. If she had given him that dose, he might have died. They insisted that he'd wake up soon, and lo and behold, he did.

As soon as the doctors and technicians were dismissed, we gave Sonya and Oleg a chance to catch up. Eleven years was a long time to catch up for, though, and Sonya was prepared to take it one step at a time.

"Who?" Oleg demanded after they expressed the utter joy of seeing each other again. Oleg finally stopped telling her how he'd never given up, how he'd always prayed for this day. Now, he wanted to get down to business. "Who?" he ordered again, scowling.

"Easy, Boss," Lev warned, holding his hand up. "No stress."

Oleg didn't spare him a glance, focused on Sonya. "Who took you?"

"Someone who will pay," Sonya replied diplomatically and calmly.

"Of course, they'll fucking pay. Whoever dared to take you will feel the wrath of the Baranov might and—"

"*Easy*," she scolded, firm but gentle. "I'll have you know you were almost killed today—twice. Your heart is recovering. I may not know all the details about what's been happening with your health yet, but I am confident you have to listen to the doctors, to Lev. To me. Take it easy, Uncle." She leaned in to kiss his brow, holding his hand. "I am here. I am safe. And I'm never going anywhere again." Smiling more, she placed her free hand on her stomach and glanced up at me. "I can trust that my baby's father will see to it."

Okay. So that *cat is out of the bag.*

"Baby?" Vik exclaimed.

"I *told* you," Kelly insisted with a smile.

"Whose baby? From captivity?" Lev asked.

"You will have a child?" Oleg asked, wonder and joy in his eyes as he patted her hand that still held his.

"One thing at a time," Irina joked lightly.

"Yes, I'm having a baby." Sonya stood and came to lean against my side.

I wrapped my arm around her and hugged her close. "*We* are having a baby."

Lev's jaw dropped. Vik's did the same.

Oleg chuckled. "Now that's something I thought I'd die before seeing."

Lev scowled. "You're *not* dying."

"I've never seen you dumbfounded like that," Oleg teased of Lev.

Already, Lev was returning his attention to me. "Warner, you've a lot of explaining to do."

"And we will." Sonya pressed her hand to my chest, and damn if that didn't make me feel good. Every touch of her hands comforted me, grounding me with the fact that she would be mine. "We will both explain. There is so much to say and learn and catch up on. But I would rather do that at home. I want to see my sister."

We all agreed this reunion would be better accomplished at home, with Eva, and we all prepared to see what we could do about getting Oleg discharged. Even though he'd just woken up, this was the Baranov family. They'd make it happen. They'd get whatever nurses and doctors they wanted for home visits.

It was clear that no one wanted to leave Oleg unattended here. Sonya didn't. So it was with expedited arrangements that we worked on having Oleg discharged. While we waited, Sonya zeroed in on Irina, wanting to know how in the hell a Petrov princess could be within this circle of Baranovs.

I got the impression that Sonya wanted to share *her* story after she heard from everyone else. If she'd been deprived of information for so many years, I couldn't fault her for being so hungry and eager to get answers from everyone else.

Nurses came and went from the room to prepare for Oleg's departure. Doctors and techs did too. With team effort, many collaborated on getting Oleg ready to go home. The nurse who'd move into the mansion to oversee his recovery was critical in orchestrating it all. She couldn't be cheap, but the Baranovs would spare no expense for their leader.

All the while, Irina and Vik explained how they'd gotten together. Vik told her how he'd gone to the college campus to pose as a professor to get more intel out of Irina, but they both fell in love. Irina wasn't shy to admit how Igor Petrov had used her, expecting her to spy like a soldier. When Irina explained that Igor used her brother as leverage to ensure her compliance, Sonya seethed and wished the man dead.

"No one wants him dead more than *me*," Irina said hotly, crossing her arms.

"And me," Vik added before kissing the top of her head. "And we will kill him."

"If Boris hadn't died and I didn't have that heart attack," Oleg said as he waited in a wheelchair to be wheeled out of the room, "we would've been focusing more on taking him out."

"Now I understand why you would've worried at seeing me near Eva at that restaurant," Irina told Sonya as we all walked out together. "You remembered I was a Petrov."

Sonya nodded. "But no more." She smiled at Irina and Vik. "I'm glad you found each other."

"And I'm glad you helped Eva and Lev escape," Oleg said as Lev wheeled him down the hallway.

"Wait. What?" Sonya volleyed her gaze among all of them.

In the car, Irina explained more—of how she'd helped Eva and Lev escape when the Petrov and Ilyin families worked together to kill Lev. Sonya and Irina sat in the back and Vik drove us home. As I listened in, I realized Sonya would need significant time to let this all settle in. This was a condensed rush of information to take in.

Before we were halfway to the Baranov mansion, though, Vik swerved sharply.

"Fuck. Hold on!"

Cars sped past us, zooming on both sides of the SUV we were in. Multiple cars drove alongside us, and all of them shot at us.

Hunching down, I got my gun out and ready, but I didn't hesitate to glance back at Sonya.

She was alert, with a furrowed brow as she crouched over in the backseat. Both she and Irina hunkered down, trying to cover Oleg in the middle.

As Vik tried to stay on the road, speeding and swerving to avoid the other cars smacking into us, other Baranov cars fired back.

Ahead of us, Lev's SUV braked hard. The second he stopped, both he and Rurik leaned out to fire nonstop at the black car that sideswiped us.

Tires squealed as Vik tried not to go off the road. He didn't succeed. As the SUV tilted and spun, then canted to the side, we all held our breath and gripped the closest hand hold.

"Stay down," Vik ordered.

"Which motherfuckers are trying to kill me now?" Oleg grumped. "I'm getting sick of this shit." He remained lodged between Sonya and Irina as both women tried to cover him. In the backseat, they would be hard targets to hit.

The second the SUV slammed back down onto all four tires, Vik and I tried to force our doors open and shoot.

"Sonya!" I reached back, handing her a gun, just in case. Already, Petrovs were rushing at our SUV despite the barrage of gunfire from Lev and Rurik shooting at them from their stopped car.

She nodded, taking the gun and holding it up at the window, prepared in case anyone tried to open the door. No shots penetrated the bulletproof SUV, but that didn't mean the door couldn't be forced open with the damage from its crash.

"This ends now," Irina swore.

She shoved her door open, slamming it against the Petrov man trying to open it. Her action could've put Oleg at risk, but Sonya urged him to duck down further.

Irina exited the car shooting, her arms steady as she killed one man after the other. Vik managed to break his damaged door open too, and he joined her on the pavement, firing nonstop.

It was Igor's doing, and I heard the moment Irina found him among the carnage.

"Die," she screamed. "Die and know your death is at my hands"—shot—"that it is me killing you"—shot—"and that you will never control my life again"—shot—"that you will never make my brother suffer ever again!" A final shot accompanied the end of her tirade.

If I hadn't witnessed it, I might not have believed it. But it *was* done, just like she'd vowed. Irina had killed Igor Petrov. The daughter of the rival family had found him hiding behind a car, letting his men do the dirty work for him. Shot by shot, all of them aimed at his chest and the last one at his head, she'd killed her father.

That was one enemy out of the way. One chore crossed off the list of ensuring Sonya would be safe.

As Irina dropped her arm, her shoulders sagged and she heaved out a deep exhale.

She'd killed him. At last, she'd made good on her promise to end him, and she'd done so in the name of protecting the Baranovs.

"Irina." Vik approached her, letting the rest of the Baranov men stabilize the area and make sure no other Petrovs still lived from the shootout.

Vik continued toward his woman, and I stayed by the car. Checking on both Oleg and Sonya, I inventoried them carefully.

Blood marred Sonya's brow. I immediately sought her eyes, worried, and Oleg was concerned as well. He looked stable, no worse for the wear.

"I just bumped my head," Sonya said.

"Let's go back," I said. "Let's make sure—"

"Are you all right?" Oleg asked.

She shook her head at both of us. "It's just from the impact of stopping. I put my arm up too." She showed us. "Because I saw it coming. I put my arm up just in time, but the edge of the door frame still cut into my skin. I'm all right."

"Are you sure?" I had to check. Nothing would stop me from keeping her safe and healthy.

"I am sure." She nodded at me once, as if to further validate her words. "I just want to go home."

We all turned to look outside, watching Vik hold Irina close. They hugged, no doubt shaken by the enormity of what had happened.

Igor had chased us in an attempt to kill Oleg. Or all of us. In the end, a Mafia family leader had been killed—him.

Igor Petrov was no longer a threat.

"Let's go home," Oleg said as the crowd of men dispersed outside the car.

"Yes." Sonya sighed, and Irina and Vik made their way back to us. "I've waited eleven years to do just that." Locking her vulnerable gaze on me, despite her family members surrounding us, she said, "Take me home, please."

I tried my best not to get ahead of myself with the implication that she could see the Baranovs' place as where *I* could belong too, at her side.

23

SONYA

Surprisingly, the SUV got us home. It wasn't a smooth ride, and I was sure it would be taken to a junkyard after that collision. But it got us home. Oleg checked again that I was all right from that bump on my head.

"You're the one who was just in the hospital," I reminded him.

Ben turned and frowned at me. "So were *you*."

"What?" Oleg didn't rest easy until Ben and I explained how we'd come there to see him, then saved him from that Petrov soldier and that nurse.

I hoped that talking would help jar Irina out of the stupefied daze she seemed stuck in, but she remained quiet the entire ride back to the mansion I'd grown up in.

I'd dreamed of making this final return trip so many times. I'd tried to hire someone to drive me there since I escaped. And now that we were pulling into the long drive, the magic of the experience faded.

Too many other things were going on. Igor was killed. Irina had murdered her father. We'd been chased. Oleg was alive, not dead like I'd believed for so long. He survived more attempts on his life, too.

Danger was ever-present in this world, but I realized as the SUV stopped and the doors were opened that I'd been sheltered from it for years. After the Ilyins killed my mother, I'd been left alone, secluded and isolated, captive and guarded. Of course, I was in danger all that time, but not present danger.

Returning to it now felt… normal. Like what my life should be like.

Ben took my hand as we walked toward the mansion, but I kept our pace slow. No one rushed me, and I appreciated the chance to look at it all. The house was the same, yet not. Anything could look different after eleven years, but the second I walked up the steps, a deep sense of coming home hit me.

I was home.

I wasn't stuck on that property.

I was in control of my life, returning where I belonged.

A wide smile lifted my lips, and I didn't try to hide it.

"You're okay?" Ben checked, squeezing my fingers.

"I've never been better." I looked up at him, knowing this return was more complete with him at my side. I wasn't just coming home. I was starting the first step toward my future with him here.

So far, no one seemed offended or confused that I was with him. Plenty of questions had to linger about how Ben and I knew each other and when and how we'd conceived a baby. Those answers would come, but until we could sit down and discuss it all, I had every bit of faith that he would be accepted as my partner. It helped that he was already working for them, or with them. I doubted he considered himself much of an independent contractor anymore, not since he was so helpful in my uncle's room at that time of threats.

The moment we entered the house and I saw my sister, though, I cautioned myself from getting too far ahead with happiness.

Eva narrowed her eyes at me and crossed her arms. Surprise showed on her lovely face, and stubborn antagonism was evident in the line of her closed lips clamped together.

I drew in a deep breath, saddened that this was how our reunion would start.

"So, you live."

"Eva," Oleg scolded harshly at her greeting.

"Uncle?" She lost the scowl for me and looked at him with happy surprise. "You're… you're…"

"Alive as well," he grumped. "Almost killed twice today, though. He saved me." He pointed at Ben. "Then she saved me." He pointed at me and smiled. "And then she saved me too." He put his hand on Irina's back. "Which is why I'm disappointed in your acting like Sonya's return isn't something to celebrate. Taking care of this family, of the Baranov legacy we share, is priority."

He frowned but accepted Eva's hug. She really was happy that he was well and home. "I agree. And I'm sorry." She looked from him to me. "But I've spent the last eleven years hating that my mother ran away with her and didn't want me."

I cleared my throat. "The Ilyins took me and Mother. We were held captive. They killed her ten years ago, and I've plotted to escape and come home to our family every single day of those years."

Eva left Oleg and approached me slowly. "You were taken?"

I nodded, trying my best not to cry at the sight of my baby sister all grown up. We'd lost so much time, and I hated that she'd assumed something so false. She'd let such anger and resentment fester all this time. "I would never leave our family. Mother wouldn't have either."

Eva let out a cry, sobbing as she ran to me. Wrapping her arms around me, she hugged me tight. But just as quickly as she embraced me, she released me. "Wait. You *are* pregnant." She looked at Kelly and Irina. "It's really you. And you're... pregnant."

I nodded, smiling again as we hugged once more. Words could wait. I had a decade of missing hugs from her.

"And I killed my father."

That statement was Irina's, dull and blunt. She still had a dazed, vacant expression regardless of Vik standing with her and keeping his arm around her.

"What?" Eva furrowed her brow again and looked at her friend. "What did you say?"

"A *lot* has happened today," Lev summarized, almost flippantly. He kissed her and rejoined Oleg to assist him further into the house.

"Come along, Irina. Sit," the Boss urged, beckoning Irina to enter his favorite lounge with him. We all followed in, and Eva didn't leave my side.

"Am I dreaming? Is this really happening?" She frowned up at me.

I couldn't take my eyes off our uncle guiding Irina into the room. He already saw her as one of his own, a former enemy and now ally. Oleg used to rule with such an iron fist, but I'd never doubted that he had a big heart. And he proved it again now.

A teenager came into the room, signing to Irina, and she responded with gestures as well.

"That's Maxim," Eva explained. "He's—oh. You've got a lot to catch up on."

I nodded then tipped my chin at Irina. "But given how shaken up she seems, I think we need to start with what happened today and work backward."

Eva smiled, a real one, and hugged me close before I sat with Ben. "I am so glad you are home."

I arched a brow. "And that I hadn't run away?"

A shameful frown covered her face, but I wasn't going to allow that. I hadn't come home to hold a grudge. "Eva, relax. My disappearance couldn't have been a simple thing to explain or understand. We'll talk."

With one more nod, she moved over toward Lev as the family gathered for a meeting.

"Igor Petrov had a soldier attempt to smother me at the hospital," my uncle began. "And the Ilyins paid off a nurse to kill me as well. On the way home, Igor joined his men in an attempt to run us off the road and opened gunfire." He patted Irina's knee, as she sat next to him, Vik at her other side. "Irina approached in kind and killed him." Lifting his chin, he almost smiled. "The Petrov family will disintegrate and will no longer be a threat to the Baranovs."

We all sat in silence, deferring to him.

Then, loudly and awkwardly, someone reacted in a shout. "Oh, thank fuck."

We all turned toward Maxim, who was deaf. It was a blunt reply that none of us would judge him for. It sounded like Igor had abused and neglected the boy, and he likely had every right to be glad the man was dead.

I smiled, looking forward to meeting and getting to know him more. Countless surprises might be waiting for me as I reacclimate to being home, but acquainting myself with a new half-brother would be a joy.

"Now the Ilyins need to be dealt with," Ben said.

Oleg raised his brows. "And since when have you become a member of this family, Mr. Warner? Before the wedding, I was under the impression that you were nothing but an independent hitman we wanted to hire for a hit on O'Malley."

"I was," Ben replied.

"But he's now the father of my child." I didn't stutter, proud to claim this connection. "And he *will* be in this family."

Lev huffed a single laugh, amused. It looked like he'd need to get over whatever initial hangups he'd had about Ben. With how sneaky Ben could be, I bet there were a few instances where Lev struggled to let him close to the family.

Not anymore. Ben *was* my family. I couldn't state anything about our marrying, but he didn't seem to want to leave my side ever again. Nor did I want to leave his. We were in this together.

"The Ilyins took her and her mother," Ben added. "And I will seek revenge on the men who dared to hurt the mother of my child."

"And what happened to…" Oleg lowered his face, seeming to lose his courage to continue.

"They killed her," I stated, trying my best to keep the heavy emotions out of my tone. "They attempted to rape me, and when she fought them, they raped her and killed her instead."

No one spoke, and as I watched the fury on my uncle's face, I regretted being so direct like that. He shouldn't be exposed to stress. He had to take it easy. He'd had a heart attack, and here I was giving him hard, gruesome news that would invoke rage.

"Those motherfuckers," he growled. He ranted on, cursing more in Russian, and we all jumped into action, telling him to calm down.

"The Petrovs and Ilyins," he growled once he sat again and seemed slightly calmer. "Both of them had always been trying to knock our family down. Back then and now."

"And now they're making it easier," Ben said, speaking up. "The Ilyins schemed to take Sonya so she would grow up and marry Eric Benson."

Oleg pounded his fist on the armrest of his chair. "I knew that fucking Benson had something to do with it. I searched for clues for years. Back then, he'd been obsessed over reducing my power, about culling the might of the Baranov name."

Ben nodded, getting up to pace. "Geoff Ilyin admitted that they'd taken Sonya so they could arrange a marriage between a Baranov and a Benson. That way, when Eric was in office and had political power, he'd be able to use his leverage as having Sonya as his wife."

"Of course. He'd rule against us," Oleg guessed. "And he would be 'family'."

"Geoff intended to court his favor," Ben added.

"And Igor must have realized they'd be squeezed out as a power," Vik said. "Hence his desperation to kill Oleg."

Lev crossed his arms, looking like a warrior. "Then all that remains is taking out the Ilyins."

"You up for it?" Ben taunted.

Lev scowled at him.

"The Petrovs will fall apart," Irina stated, seeming calmer the more we all talked.

"And once we go after the Ilyins," Lev said, "no threats will remain."

"The Baranovs will rule in peace," Rurik said from the side where he stood with Kelly.

"No. Not in peace," Kelly said. "*I will never be at peace until O'Malley is killed.*"

The men all looked at Ben.

He sighed. "I'm on it. I was a little sidetracked when I crossed paths with Sonya…"

"And Benson," I added. "I won't relax until I know my so-called *intended* is dead."

"Benson and O'Malley," Oleg said, pointing at Lev and Ben. "You two handle them." Then addressing Vik and Rurik, he said, "And you two gather the men to annihilate the Ilyins once and for all."

Looking at me, then Irina, and lastly, Kelly, Oleg smiled calmly. "It is already time to prepare for the next generation of Baranovs to come. And I want them to have the security and safety they deserve."

24

BEN

"You're pregnant too?" Sonya asked Irina. Then she looked at Kelly. "And you?"

Both women nodded.

"We'll fill you in about all that," Eva said, quickly getting over her hesitation about her sister returning. She had been so standoffish at first, but while we all talked in this lounge, I watched her. She couldn't stop looking at Sonya, as though she doubted her eyes. The slow and tenuous smile on her face proved she was giving up on any grudges she might have held against her sister. With Sonya's explanation of how she had been taken, Eva had no grounds to be rude or think something false about her. I hadn't gotten to know Eva that well, but she seemed like an understanding person. I was happy there wouldn't be any issues between the sisters when Sonya had been so eager to return to Eva and was so worried about her needing protection.

"This matter of the Ilyins is most important to deal with, and now." Oleg firmed his lips in a stern line. Looking again at me and Lev, he added, "It shouldn't take two hitmen long to kill a couple of corrupt politicians."

"Well, I can't speak for him," I said teasingly, "but—"

"Oh, shut up." Lev scoffed. "You said you had a hit for Yusef Ilyin too. And who was the one who actually killed him? Me, that's right."

I rolled my eyes. "But—"

"Enough," Oleg ordered. "I have yet to speak with you privately, Mr. Warner. But should I officially welcome you to this family, you will abide by my rules. The first of which includes not annoying me with bickering among your brothers."

Brothers. It had been a very long time since I could use that word about myself. I used to have brothers in the Bratva that rejected me and my brother. I used to have brothers in the military as well.

All this time, I thought being solo and independent suited me best. With the easygoing teasing that Lev and I seemed to enjoy in a game of one-upping each other, I felt like I was really finding my place in the world. I grew more confident that the Baranovs were the ones I should stand with. And I'd be damned proud to contribute to and protect their legacy.

"Understood," I replied, meaning it.

"At least we've already done a thorough background check on him to know he's not an enemy," Rurik quipped dryly.

"Thanks," I retorted.

Oleg pointed at me. "You and I will speak later."

I nodded, not having any intention to screw up my "welcome" here. I'd dealt with Lev and the others so far, not Oleg, but he wasn't scaring me off yet. Even if the Baranov Boss didn't want me included in this inner circle, I would never leave Sonya's side.

"You and Lev can handle Benson and O'Malley," he repeated, "and then you can join Vik and Rurik with the men to end the Ilyins once and for all." Shaking his head, he sighed then rubbed his brow.

"Are you all—"

Sonya and Eva started to ask the same question in unison, then laughed.

"Are you okay?" Kelly asked instead.

He nodded. "It's just a damn shame it had to come to this. Geoff's cousin, Nicholas, was supposed to marry Amelia."

Eva gasped and Sonya furrowed her brow. "My mother?" Eva asked.

Oleg nodded. "They were arranged to be engaged, I think in part because my father wanted to have me marry someone else for an alliance. I saw through that plan and I knew that alliance wouldn't last. And it didn't help that Amelia and I fell in love." He sighed, a heavy sound full of regret. "I tried to do my best to keep her away from the Ilyins, not wanting that fate for her. I was suspicious then that the Ilyins were scheming to take us down, and my father was too ignorant or blind to notice it.

"Amelia also didn't want to end up with Nicholas. I was already promised to another, but I suggested that she try to become a Baranov anyway, for the sake of her safety. And so… she met Boris."

"And never loved him," Sonya guessed.

Oleg shook his head. "She never wanted to marry him, but she wanted our friendship to last. She wanted to be in the Baranov family, no other. That was the beginning of the Ilyins' big upset with us. They believed we'd taken 'their bride.'"

"Then they took Sonya as payback?" Eva guessed.

Oleg nodded. "That was my first guess. And I looked far and wide for a clue that would indicate that. But I found no trace of them. Nothing."

"I was held on a property far north, upstate," Sonya said.

"And they covered their tracks well, for many years," Oleg admitted. "At that time of the marriages, though, Benson started to get involved. He'd made it clear that he wanted to back a Mafia family and lean on one for protection, but he tried to play them all, keeping them guessing who was his favorite. If Geoff had Sonya marry Eric Benson, they'd use that marriage as a way to ensure they could reduce our power and have the Ilyins rise in power and wealth."

Corruption ran rife with these families.

"That won't happen," Sonya vowed. "I won't marry him. I will not be used as a pawn." As she lowered her gaze, she let out a troubled breath. "I lost too many years of my life in captivity as it is."

"I won't let that happen. I'll kill Eric."

"And O'Malley," Lev reminded me.

Obviously. I nodded, though, refraining from tossing a retort back at him.

"We won't lose you again," Eva swore, looking at Sonya with deep care and compassion burning in her gaze.

"You were already hired for O'Malley, weren't you?" Oleg looked from me to Lev, as if he expected confirmation of that. "Or we were in the process of finding you for that job?"

"Yes. I was on task for O'Malley, but once I realized who Sonya was and that we—"

"You know what?" Eva stood, encouraging Sonya to rise with her. "Why don't we let the men have their time to speak? Ben can explain more. You and I, though" —she guided Sonya toward the door— "have more to talk about, *Sister*."

Sonya glanced at me, smiling. "All right." As she passed by Lev, she narrowed her eyes at him. "Be nice, *Brother*."

He rolled his eyes.

Irina and Kelly exited the room as well, and Maxim trailed out after Irina, signing something.

Left in the room with the upper men of the Baranov family, I braced myself for getting down to business.

Before anyone else could speak, Oleg studied me sternly. "What are your intentions with Sonya?"

"Right out of the gate with that question, huh?"

He scowled, expecting an answer.

I plan to be with her. To love her. To love on her. To raise a child with her. To protect her and make sure she never has to feel like she's in the dark or powerless or trapped.

"I plan to be with her—however she'll let me into her life."

"And you will swear your loyalty to the Baranov name as well?" he asked.

I shoved my hands in my pockets. "Maybe I already did a while back. I've never taken on a hit to kill or capture any member of your family."

"Why not?" Vik asked.

"Because you seemed like the only decent ones around. I was sick of the Petrovs and Ilyins. I was waiting for them to cancel each other out."

"Why would you care one way or another, as an independent?" Rurik asked.

I shrugged. "Because I'm tired of being solo. I'd been thinking about slowing down and finding a group to belong to for a while."

"So you saw Sonya and decided to get a head start on a making a family?" Lev huffed, still doubtful of me and my intentions. "Something doesn't add up here. How the hell did you even meet her if she was captive all this time?"

I'd been expecting this discussion. "I took a hit to kill an Ilyin, someone within their organization. It was a hit placed by a Cartel. From tracking that Ilyin down, I ended up near the property Sonya must have been held at. She showed up at a bar one night, sneaking out and escaping because she wanted to lose her virginity. She said she knew she couldn't get away. Every time she tried to, someone in the small town alerted the Ilyins and she was recaptured, but she snuck out to hook up with someone—anyone. And…" I shrugged. They didn't need me to spell out the obvious. "I was intrigued by a beautiful stranger and we became acquainted that night." That was putting it mildly. I then explained how she'd run away and I thought I'd never see her again. How I couldn't stop thinking about her.

"We agreed to no details. Just strangers hooking up. But after I came to the wedding and—"

Lev growled. "You snuck into my wedding?"

"Yeah. You'd been reaching out to me about a hit, and I wanted a better feel for who you are before I considered taking it. I like to be thorough and deliberate with my research and I only take jobs I truly stand by. When Boris died that night, I was on edge." I faced Oleg. "Because Igor had previously tried to hire me to kill you. When I showed no interest in the job or his offer, it sounds like he went to someone else."

Rurik nodded. "That sounds right. The men who shot at him at the warehouse were sloppy."

"Then when Boris died," I said, "I wondered if someone else was acting on hits aimed at your family. I wanted to know who my competition might be. So, I went to spy on Igor and Geoff meeting up, and that's when they talked about ending you. That's where I heard Sonya's name, and I got curious whether they could be talking about my stranger upstate."

They listened as I went on, sharing how I'd eventually followed O'Malley to that strip club and how Sonya had run there from next door. Telling them that we'd fucked again wasn't necessary. But I slowly brought them all up to speed until the events of today.

I gave them a chance to absorb it all. Eventually, after a few moments of silence, Vik spoke up. "You killed a whole crew of Ilyins to save her?"

"I wasn't counting how many." I shrugged again. "It didn't matter how many. All that matters is that they're dead."

Rurik nodded. "Yeah, I like him." He walked up to me and shook my hand. "Welcome to the family."

"This is official?" Lev asked Oleg. "He's in? Just like that?"

The Boss huffed. "I doubt you'll get him to stay away from Sonya if he's already gone so far to prove his commitment to protecting her." With something that looked like a smile, he eyed me. "Welcome, Ben. I appreciate your diligence in keeping my niece safe."

"That's it? I'm... initiated?" It seemed so simple.

"Yes," Oleg said. "And now it's time to remove all the threats hanging over us."

Count me in. Mentally, I was already on it.

I couldn't wait to end the men who posed pending trouble for my woman and our baby.

25

SONYA

Eva led me up to the second floor, and I assumed she was taking me toward my former room. After the stress of coming closer to home, seeing Oleg almost killed, then the worry of having my baby checked out after spotting blood, I'd been put through the wringer.

I would love to lie down and rest. A nap would be heavenly. But I didn't want to put off catching up with my sister.

"Your room isn't the same anymore," she warned. "A small fire happened about seven years ago, and a few rooms on this side of the house were damaged."

I shrugged, unbothered. My room would be something familiar, but I didn't need it to ground me. Things were replaceable. Material items couldn't matter that much after what I'd gone through. In captivity, I learned what really mattered—having the people I loved, my family.

As we entered the room now decorated as a guest suite, I took in the differences. Memories lingered in the back of my mind and I could see what it used to look like, but I wasn't suffering a sense of loss at my room not being the same as what I recalled. Reconciling the *then* and *now* wasn't painful.

And why would it be? I didn't want to go back in time. I had no desire to linger in the past. I wasn't the same young teenager I was when I'd been taken, and the items and décor that comforted me then wouldn't hold the same value now. I valued my life, my baby, my future, and Eva seemed pleased that I wasn't upset.

"Want me to give you a minute?" she asked gently.

"No," Irina said bluntly as she and Kelly came in as well. "There is way too much to catch up on."

I had a hunch I'd like this woman. "Maybe let me shower? Then we can talk some more."

Kelly called up food, and while I showered and cleaned up, they set up a little early dinner in the dining area of the suite.

Showering felt good, but while I was under the spray of warm water, I wondered how Ben was faring with the others. I didn't doubt him. He'd stand his own, but I knew he could very well be counting down the seconds until he'd be at my side again, just the same as I was looking forward to relaxing with him here.

Once I was dressed and relaxed, I joined Eva, Irina, and Kelly. For hours, we caught up through tears and laughter, with hard explanations and many questions. We still had a lot more to catch up on. Eleven years was a long time. Mostly, it was me and Eva speaking, but it wasn't intrusive for Irina and Kelly to be there.

Being home was overwhelming, but in a good way. I was so content to be within these four walls again, and I embraced how full my heart felt. Irina and Kelly were welcome additions to the family I'd missed, and I was grateful they'd be there to comfort me too.

Well after the sun had set, Kelly noticed me yawning more frequently. "Maybe we can resume this tomorrow."

I nodded, glad she was ready for a break. "I am tired."

"I can only imagine," Eva said.

We promised to catch up tomorrow, and they left. No sooner had they filed out of the room than Ben entered.

"How did it go?" I asked him once he closed and locked the door.

"Fine." He strode further into the room, shedding his clothes as he went. Aiming for me on the bed, he made his intentions clear.

Just like I'd imagined, he was impatient with this distance between us. Now that he was here and staring at me with that hungry gaze, all my fatigue faded. I was alert, with my blood coursing through me faster, pushing my desire higher. My heart thumped quicker, increasing my excitement. Since I'd only put on loungewear that the other women had found for me to borrow until I got my own things, I felt exposed as it was. No bra or panties. Just soft, thin terrycloth.

When I sat up and climbed to my knees, never taking my gaze off his, I reached for the hem of my shirt.

"No." He tossed his shirt aside and unzipped his pants. "Let me." A gentle push of his fingers on my shoulder urged me to fall back onto the bed, and I smiled up at him. Relaxing was the last thing on my mind as he leaned down over me. As he slowly and deeply kissed me, full of need and demand, he pulled off my clothes.

All that was on my mind was *him*.

"I can't wait another minute to finally see all of you." He kneeled back on the bed, rising up so he could rake his gaze over me. Feasting his eyes on every naked inch of my body, he growled and lowered his hand to rub along my folds.

"You've seen me," I replied breathily.

"Not like this. Relaxed. Safe. Without a worry about returning home or someone trying to kill you."

I laughed lightly as he pressed his fingers deeper, penetrating me with a wicked lightness. I wanted him to pound into me and fill me like he did before. I wanted the friction and the grind. He was teasing, and I accepted it, knowing he'd treat me so well.

"Someone will *always* be trying to kill me. That's part and parcel of being a Baranov."

"And when you're a Warner, too," he added.

Hold on. Did he mean when *I* was a Warner, as in he planned to make this official between us with marriage? Or did he mean he was a Warner and he could sympathize?

"You're thinking too much," he taunted, lowering to kiss me again.

I gave up deciphering what he'd said and resorted to only feeling him. All of him. His drugging kisses and the stroke of his tongue alongside mine. His hands so callused and firm as they kneaded and teased my breasts. His fingers returning to my pussy where he swiped them through the wetness I couldn't stop him from finding. This rugged man would never fail to arouse me, and it was a sweet surrender to lie back and accept it.

As he pulled back from kissing my lips, he trailed wet, hot kisses down my neck until he could suck on my nipples. I arched up, alert and surprised. "Oh!"

"Sensitive?" he teased with a naughty smirk. Still, he kissed and played with me, turning me on until I'd be on the edge of begging him to let me come. And that was just from foreplay alone. He truly was proving to be the master of my body.

"Very sensitive." I spread my legs further apart, pushing my hips up to encourage him to focus on me there.

"Patience," he chided.

"I don't want to be patient."

"But you can be. We will have all the time in the world to make love."

I smiled, watching him as he kissed my baby bump. "Love?"

He locked his intense stare on me as he crawled further down the bed. "Yeah. Because that's it—you're it—for me. I love you, Sonya."

"And I love you, Ben." Damn, did it feel so good to say it. As sudden as it happened, it was right. "And I will never stop being grateful that you've saved me. In more ways than one."

He lowered his face between my legs, kissing around my pussy as he gripped the undersides of my thighs. "And I'll never stop being grateful that you've saved me too. That you've shown me where I belong, what my purpose is."

At the first touch of his tongue on my clit, then his warm lips pressing against me and sucking, I hoped he didn't intend to keep this conversation going. I couldn't reply. Only with moans and pushing my hips up into his face as he licked and sucked at me. Those were my replies. In the show of his actions, loving me and pleasuring me, I didn't need to ask for clarification of what he thought his purpose was.

He pushed me to come too soon. With cries of euphoria, I trembled and lay on the bed. Yet my heart was soaring, my soul was free, and I felt like I was on cloud nine.

Before I could catch my breath, I registered the dips on the mattress of his climbing back up over me. Hovering like a ravenous beast, his chin still shining with my juices, he lined his big, thick cock up to my entrance.

"I'm going to love you until the end of my days," he vowed.

I nodded, too breathless to speak. When he nudged the tip of his dick inside me, I lost any ability to form a sentence, much less say it.

"I'm going to be a father for our child." He drove in all the way, culminating his thrust with a deep growl and dropping his head back.

Still as he slammed into me with force, pushing me close to coming again, he kept up his promises for the future. Seeing him staring right back let me *feel* the sincerity of his words. This wasn't nonsense he spewed in the heat of the moment. As he dragged along my inner walls, already so stretched and sensitive to him, he told the truth. "I'm going to marry you and make sure the whole world knows they won't be able to harm you. Ever again."

I cried out as I came, clenching his big dick.

"Fuck," he whispered as he jerked once more. By the twitching of his shaft so deep inside me, we'd reached our release at the same time. Jerking slightly, he spilled his hot cum in me, and I relished the contraction of my orgasm as I milked him dry.

"I love you," he said again, catching his breath as he lowered to me on the mattress. Without pulling his cock out of me, he rolled us so we'd face each other on our sides. The second he settled against me, he framed my face. I kissed him, swearing back all the sentiment that he'd shared.

"I love you too," I whispered, kissing him again and holding him tight. "And I always will."

I wasn't only home by being back in this house after captivity. I was home in the sense of my heart being full. With him.

26

BEN

Over the next couple of days, many things happened.

Sonya and I practically moved into the big mansion where she'd grown up. I disclosed all my properties, and Oleg tasked a soldier with checking on them. The idea was that should anyone learn that I was now a Baranov brother, someone could try to break in and set traps or listening devices.

We all continued to catch up and explain what was going on and what we'd pieced together. There was a wealth of things that still needed to be said, especially from Sonya's experiences, but she dismissed Eva's concerns.

"Of course, I will need help to overcome the trauma," Sonya said at breakfast on the third day of her return. "I anticipate looking into getting therapy and whatever else might help me process healthily. But right now, other things are more pressing." She rested her hand on her stomach and smiled that contented smile that never failed to steal my breath. Seeing her happy made me happy. "Like preparing for this one to come. And that preparation includes killing our enemies."

No other woman would ever be as perfect for me as she was, shrewd when she needed to be and gentle otherwise. She understood the urgency of going after Eric Benson. She wasn't shocked that killing Benson included taking out O'Malley since they worked together so much. And she wasn't one bit nervous or guilty about the Baranov forces plotting to eliminate the Ilyins.

Lev and I set out to handle our task first. While Eva, Irina, and Kelly helped Sonya continue to adjust to being home, I left with Lev to take out Benson and O'Malley. When we exited the house, I smiled at the scene behind us. Sonya was all smiles to get to know Maxim more, and that was what she was doing last, talking and learning to sign to communicate with him.

"Did Vik and Rurik leave already?" I asked as Lev and I got into an SUV. We weren't taking any backup. Neither of us needed it, and the fewer, the better in this regard for this mission.

"Yes," he replied. A deep rumble of thunder cut through the quiet that followed his response. A storm was brewing. With the increase of pressure in the air, it suited the mood of the afternoon. Solemn, ominous, and foreboding.

"Are you ready?" he asked as he started the car.

"Of course."

"I can tell that you want to spend more time with Sonya and make sure she's settling in well," Lev said, almost conversationally, "but this shouldn't wait."

"No," I agreed. "It can't wait. I hate that it's been this difficult to pull off all along." I hadn't been hired to kill Benson, but O'Malley. Still, if I hadn't been on a side quest looking for Sonya, I would've been more frustrated at how long this was taking to kill the governor elect.

"I know what you mean. But it's nothing you can control. Too many protestors are making security a constant for both Benson and O'Malley."

"Yeah." I nodded as I watched the scenery outside. I'd since learned that the shootout at the strip club was because of one particular protest group. An environmental group didn't like how the incoming politicians were planning to behave in office, and they took matters into their own hands and tried to assassinate them.

Too bad they didn't succeed.

"We'll finish it today," Lev said.

Again, I nodded.

"And with this first assignment, I hope you understand that we are officially offering you a job."

I grunted a laugh. "No, really?" I joked. Then I shook my head. "I appreciate the offer, as implied as it already was, but I plan to settle down with Sonya and have a family. For the first time in a long time, I want to focus on my family."

"You have one now, with the Baranovs."

I nodded. "I know, but I mean me, Sonya, and our baby." I couldn't help but smile. "It's been a pipe dream."

Lev glanced at me as he drove. "You've always thought you were a loner and now you're realizing you're not?"

"No." I sighed and decided Lev and I could be friends one day if I tried to not irritate him. Opening up to him felt right. "I was rejected from my Bratva family as a child, in Russia. My mother brought me back to the States, and I eventually joined the military. That didn't suit me either since I never truly felt like I had my place there, either." I shrugged, hating how I'd struggled to know my purpose and place. Perhaps it took the idea that I'd soon be turning forty and I needed to retreat from killing slightly to secure a family in order to have a purpose.

"I understand."

I looked at him and furrowed my brow. "You can? You're familiar with being rejected and lost?"

"Yeah." As he went on to explain his backstory, that he had been an orphan until he saved Oleg's life and was taken into the Baranov family, I realized he could say that he understood. He'd lived through that feeling of not having a place too.

We neared the Benson estate, and we shelved the talk about our pasts. It was game time, and almost in sync, we grew more alert and ready. This was time to focus and execute. Lev was no slouch with taking out hits, and I appreciated that he could be an ally. A friend in the future.

A brother.

After he parked, we exited the car and fell into a perfect partnership. I didn't have to worry whether he knew what to do, and likewise, he innately seemed to trust that I'd have his back and concentrate on my role.

No guards stopped us from entering the big house way outside the city, but that didn't surprise us. This location was harder to find, one house among many that the Benson family owned. Because it was remote and the ownership was hidden under layers of deeds, it was far from common knowledge that this country house was somewhere the Bensons could call home.

The second Lev and I stepped inside, another sharp crack of thunder struck outside, and a low, growling rumble followed. Vibrations from the thunder rose up from the floor as we strode further into the house.

Guns raised and at the ready, we progressed inside. With nods and silent, careful steps, we snuck in.

And the scene we ultimately found wasn't one I bet he expected. I sure hadn't.

"What in the fuck...?" Lev uttered it silently as he scoped out the massive, round study. Bookcases lined all the walls, and with the wood on all surfaces, the masculine room seemed dim with the storm raging outside.

Plenty of light remained for us to see the dead bodies.

Ford Benson, Eric's father, lay sprawled out on the navy carpet. He died on his back, his lifeless eyes staring unseeing at the ceiling. Several bullet holes showed clearly on his chest. Ripped white fabric denoted where he'd been shot, and the profuse spread of crimson on the pure-white garment indicated how quickly and severely he must have bled out.

Across from him, seated in the huge leather chair behind a massive mahogany desk, was Eric Benson. Or what remained of him. The bottom of his head showed where a gun had been fired upward beneath his chin. Brain matter and blood were splattered behind him from the fatal shot.

The suicidal shot.

As Lev remained on edge, gun up and checking to see if anyone else was here, I approached the desk. The only item on it, other than Eric's limp arm and the gun that was still loosely in his grip, was a paper.

I leaned over, not touching anything and disturbing evidence, and read it.

"Killed himself," I announced.

"No shit?" Lev asked.

I nodded, skimming the handwritten letter quickly. "He vowed to kill his father for pushing him into a life he didn't want. This claims he's suffered from depression all his life and hated his father for refusing to let him treat it, because that would signal a weakness and no Benson was weak. He couldn't make himself be a puppet for his father, not in office, and he refused to go through with the plans his father and O'Malley expected of him."

Finished summarizing the letter, I looked up at Lev.

"Damn," he said, deadpan.

I smiled. "Looks like we're not needed here."

Eric was no longer a threat. I couldn't wait to tell Sonya.

"No. Not here," Lev replied. "Let's go find O'Malley."

"And then we can help kill the Ilyins," I replied.

"Every one of them we can find," he growled.

Together, we left the scene of such grisly death. Someone else could find them and handle it. They were no longer a Baranov concern. They were no longer my concern.

Lev and I got back into the car, and as he drove off, heading toward O'Malley's office, I prepared to face a tougher fight this time. O'Malley would be covered by security, but he wouldn't be able to hide any longer. It wasn't just me chasing after him, but Lev, too. The governor-elect had the wrath of too many people hedged against him to survive for long.

"You good?" Lev asked when he must have noticed I was quiet.

"Of course. You?"

He nodded.

"It's just different not doing this alone," I admitted.

"I bet not." Then, uncharacteristically, he smiled. "But I'm damned glad you're on board with us."

I was. Not just for the Baranov name, but for Sonya's safety. For her peace.

And for the future our baby deserved.

"Me too. So step on it," I urged.

I couldn't wait for the rest of my life to start after this kill.

27

SONYA

Even though Eva, Irina, and Kelly kept me company all day, I couldn't ignore that the love of my life was out on a mission to kill the fiancé I never wanted.

Life couldn't get more twisted than that.

"Sonya?" Irina asked when Eva and Kelly went to get some more snacks for us from the kitchen. With how crappy it looked outside, rainy and gloomy, we made the big living room our spot. Numerous skylights should've made the space more open and airy. The many lights we had on worked to liven up the room, though.

"Hmm?" I glanced at the former Petrov. She'd killed her father a couple of days ago, and just like a Mafia princess was expected to be, she was over it. I supposed a lifetime of loathing her parent made her accept her actions faster and with relief.

"You okay?"

I nodded. "Just thinking about Ben."

She almost smiled, wryly. "Worrying, you mean?" She nodded, as if answering her own question. "I am too, about Vik."

Her fiancé was heading after the Ilyins with Rurik and several other Baranov soldiers.

"Kind of silly, huh?" I idly rubbed my stomach, finding the motion so comforting even though I didn't have much of a noticeable bump. Irina didn't either, and she was right about the stage that I was in pregnancy, give or take a few days or so.

"What's silly?"

I flicked my finger between us. "Worrying about them. We grew up with this. We learned that this is how life goes. That there is always a chance for danger and violence."

"Yes, but it's *them*. It hits so much closer to the heart when it's *our* men out there risking their lives."

"It is. But they've also grown up with this, too. They're no naïve amateurs. They're professionals." Ben was an elite professional, a skilled and experienced hitman. "But," I said, sighing, "it is harder."

"Because they matter so much more," she replied. "Because we can't imagine our lives without them."

I refuse. I'd only just started my life, the one I should've had all along. I'd be damned if Ben died on me before we actually started.

"Hey, that reminds me." I got up and walked over to a side table to grab some paper. "I need to send a letter."

Irina huffed a laugh. "A letter. How old-fashioned of you."

I ignored her teasing and began what would likely be the first draft of a letter to the Petersons. I thanked them and explained the vague details of why I couldn't tell them who I was and why I'd taken their truck. Once Oleg woke from his nap, I'd have him send a hefty thank-you gift. Depositing it in an account with an untraceable large sum would be an ideal way to pay them back for saving my life and giving me a chance to get home.

Kelly rushed back into the room without Eva. Her face was pale and her eyes were wide open. Immediately, I set the pen down and stood, furrowing my brow as I studied her. "Kelly? What's wrong?"

She lifted her hand. It shook as she showed us her phone. "I... I..." She forced a hard swallow. "I just got a call."

Thunder boomed, and we all flinched at the loud sound.

"What call?" Irina got up, joining me in reaching her across the room.

Right then, Eva showed up in the doorway, her arms full of bags of food and more beverages for us so we could continue lounging and relaxing. Neither would be happening based on how freaked out Kelly seemed.

"Whoa. Hey. What's going on?" She frowned, looking at each of us. Her expression deepened with more worry as she focused on Kelly. "Kel?" Setting the food and beverages down, she hurried toward us.

"I just got a call," Kelly repeated in that shaky, scared tone. "I got a call."

I shook my head, showing her this freak-out thing wasn't going to roll with me. Gripping her upper arms and forcing her to look at me, commanding her to ground herself and make eye contact, I ducked to level with her gaze. "Kelly. Breathe. Who called? What is it?"

More thunder boomed, and she slightly flinched this time. "A soldier."

"One of ours?" Eva asked, standing at my side.

Kelly nodded, but it turned into a shake. "Yeah. A soldier."

"Was it a Baranov?" I asked. It was or wasn't. I wondered if she knew.

"It had to be." She sobbed, covering her mouth with her free hand. "He said Rurik was killed."

I looked at Eva quickly, seeing the same instant doubt on her face. "Kelly, who called? What was his name?"

"I don't know!" Panic clung to her every word and hitched breath as she practically hyperventilated. "I don't know. He just said Rurik was killed in the fight against the Ilyins."

I shook my head again. "No. Kelly. A soldier wouldn't— No. They would identify themselves and, no. Just calm down. Who called?"

"I don't know," she sobbed again. "He's dead."

"You don't know that," Eva said.

Kelly shook out of my grasp and walked away.

"Kelly, you don't know that." I didn't walk after her since Eva was already there. Irina and I exchanged a worried glance.

"I do! I was just told!" Kelly insisted.

"It could be a ploy," I said.

Eva nodded, gesturing for Kelly to give her the phone. "We'll trace it."

"What if it's not a ploy? What if it's true? What if it's real?" She dropped to sit on the couch, then shot right back up to stand. "What if I've lost my husband? What if—"

"What if it's a ploy?" I replied loudly and firmly so she'd have no choice but to hear me.

Kelly hadn't been born in this life. She wasn't as versed with how things could go. Yes, she'd married Rurik and she was learning, but she had to get a thicker skin and gain some healthy skepticism we Mafia princesses had.

"I need to go find him. I need to see with my own eyes—"

Eva grabbed her arm as Kelly tried to run out of the room. "No. You're not."

"Soldiers don't just call a wife," Irina said. "There is protocol and—"

"No!" Kelly screamed. "I need to know if my husband is dead!"

I grabbed my phone and called Ben. Irina did the same, probably calling Vik for confirmation. Eva continued talking Kelly down from her panic, but it didn't help when none of the men could be reached. I tried Lev. Then Ben again. Even some of the other upper soldiers who I knew went with Rurik and Vik against the Ilyins.

No one answered.

But that didn't mean anything. Today was intended to be a complicated and stressful day of lots of bloodshed as our enemies were eliminated. That was why Oleg was resting. A nap was best for him while he still recovered from his ordeal.

"Kelly, we will all stay here and wait. Word will come. And you have to consider this could be a trick, a trap, or a—"

The lights cut out. The hum of the fans and air units in the house died down. It was already dark with the storm out there, but now, no light shone to cut through the bleakness in here.

The power was down.

I caught my sister's gaze, knowing this had to be deliberate. This wasn't some little house. This mansion was state-of-the-art, equipped with generators if a storm were to sever a line.

Someone's here.

I nodded at her, knowing that she'd understand without a word.

She dipped her chin once in reply, herding Kelly back toward the couch. "Come on. Irina, let's sit together."

She would keep them there.

I ran off to grab a gun.

It didn't matter that I'd only been living in this house for a few days again.

I was defiantly devoted to my family and always would be.

If someone dared to break in here, they'd have to get past me.

28

BEN

"Dammit. I've got no reception," I told Lev.

I wanted to always be accessible to Sonya if she would ever need to reach me. Lots of things were happening today, and lots of things could go wrong. That was just the nature of this life.

Lev checked his phone as we pulled into the lot for O'Malley's offices. "I don't either. Fuck. I hate that."

"This damn storm," I muttered. The rain had stopped for a while, but with how gray the sky remained, more would come. It was windier, with trees whipping branches to and fro, and it looked nasty out there. Losing reception on a night like this wasn't shocking.

"We'll make it quick," Lev said.

I hoped so. In and out. Between the two of us, a bullet had to hit the older man and end the threat he posed. No other politician would ever be in the position to meddle with the Baranovs again. Just the mere thought of that urged me into action.

Lev parked and we both hurried out. We didn't run, but we were incapable of walking or going at a slow pace. I had my fingers wrapped around my gun but I kept it in my pocket. Lev did the same. Like primed and revved-up predators on the chase, we were committed to hunting this man down.

"Shit." Lev gritted his teeth and started to jog.

I saw the same thing that triggered him. Across the parking lot, O'Malley exited the office building. In a long black coat that flapped in the wind, he held his hands up to shield his face from the gusts. As he walked away from the office building, he spoke with an Ilyin leader. It wasn't Geoff, but someone I recognized as an upper supervisor within their organization.

It didn't matter who he was. He was going down—now. He was a dead man. So were the two Ilyins walking behind them.

I jogged with Lev, bringing my gun up.

Perhaps that was our mistake, running to get to O'Malley before we'd lose this chance. In a pursuit with the urgency of *now or never*, we gave away our location with our footsteps.

"Get down," one of the guards said, shoving at O'Malley. "Get down!"

Lev was either more impatient than me or he didn't care. He lifted his hand to shoot. I was more the kind to move with stealth, to measure and strike with planning. Then again, this was an ambush. No plans applied there.

The Ilyins reacted in kind. They shot back, forcing me and Lev to pause at a concrete half-wall and duck. We took turns covering for each other as we leaned up to shoot.

Even though we didn't make it a strategy, our position was ideal. They had to pass us to reach a vehicle and flee.

Over and over, we continued to fire. We reloaded one at a time, and I bet they had as well to keep up this kind of a shootout.

Fuck. I blinked, distracted by the limitation to see.

Rain began to fall again, in such a steady stream that it was nearly impossible to see far with the deluge. Squinting and straining to fire accurately, I worried that they could get away by running along the building and give up on getting into a car.

We stayed on it, shooting at them without a break. But in facing forward, we neglected to consider anyone coming up from behind. I hadn't anticipated that they could've called for backup.

Two men jumped on us, knocking us aside with that element of surprise. Lev went down first, and this newly arrived Ilyin aimed a gun at him.

O'Malley would get away without any gunfire on him. Maybe. I couldn't determine whether I'd succeed in this shootout with limited visibility. But I could help Lev.

A shot was fired too close for comfort. The Ilyin aimed at him, but Lev rolled just in time for it to only hit his arm, not his chest.

I swung around, pointing my gun at the other man who'd arrived. A clean headshot dropped him before he could kill me.

Then as I stuck with the momentum, moving my arm in an arc, I followed through and shot the other. In that one stroke of a second, I killed him before he could put a bullet in Lev's head.

He dropped, and after checking that Lev lived, holding his hand to his arm and wincing, I pivoted to aim at O'Malley again.

Through the rain, I just barely could make him out that far away. Breathing hard as the adrenaline coursed through me, I squinted until I saw movement.

The Ilyin leader must have called for more backup. Both in those two showing up behind us and also in calling for another car to come closer to the building.

"Fuck," I muttered. "They're getting away."

"You kill those Baranovs yet?" O'Malley shouted, likely counting on the Ilyins to reply.

I fired at him as he ran for the car. That was my reply.

Lev strained to sit up next to me, but he couldn't lift his arm to join me in shooting.

"Ah, fuck you. Fuck all of you," O'Malley yelled. "I'm sick of your interference."

I fired more. He had to be hiding on the other side of the car that pulled up.

"I'll still end you. I'll end you all!"

The fuck you will.

"I'll see to it," he vowed. "Your wives and bastard children. All of them will be dead tonight."

Lev and I glanced at each other, glaring.

Neither of us would accept that threat.

"It's the end of the Baranovs," O'Malley declared. "Because none of them will survive the bombs I sent there. None of them will live to interfere with our plans again."

Bombs?

Lev tried to get up, crawling on his hands and knees until he got his feet under him.

Fuck! I guided him to move it, hurrying like I never had before.

"We need to get back to the house!" he said, dropping into a run with me.

As tires squealed on the other side of the half wall, thunder cracked then rolled. I tuned it all out, hyper focused on nothing but getting us back to the car. We moved with a mad urgency, rushing to get back and stop any bomb from killing our loved ones.

29

SONYA

I didn't get just one gun, but three.

I returned, out of breath from the exertion of running, but I refused to be distracted.

"Here." Eva whispered it, holding her hand up for me to give her one. She hunkered down on the couch with Kelly and Irina, and I didn't hesitate to back up and give her a gun. Keeping my face forward, on the biggest doorway that would lead to this room, I made sure to be on the lookout. Not looking back to see who I was handing the other gun to, I thrust my arm back and one of the women took it.

I hoped it was Irina. She knew how to shoot. She'd killed her father with precision. Kelly wasn't sobbing, crying, or panicking verbally anymore, but I knew she was already riled up from that call. She wouldn't have the level head to be able to fire a weapon at that moment.

None of us spoke, tense and listening. No one moved in the house. No sounds reached our ears. All that we could detect was the constant strum of rain pattering down on the roof. The branches knocking against the windows with the storm's rain. The low grumble of thunder.

Gripping my gun with both hands, I kept my gaze focused ahead. With this darkness of the power going out, I had to acclimate to the lack of light. And the longer I stood there, ready to defend my family, I waited for a direction of where I'd need to shoot.

I dare you.

I fucking dare you.

Whoever you are, I dare you to hurt my family.

Try to get past me again.

Try to take me again.

And I will end your life.

Repeating a mantra of firm anger and resolution, I stood tall and ready. Bracing for anything to come at us, I did my best to listen and not panic with the suspense of waiting like this.

Guards surrounded the house. Many men were here patrolling, watching the drive, manning the gate, and standing like sentinels at the doors. It wasn't just me here. It wasn't me and Eva alone. Kelly and Irina were here, and among the four of us, we would need to operate as a group.

But I knew all too well how stupid it could be to assume that having guards and a full security staff meant no harm or danger could come. I had lived through the hard lesson that even with men here for the purpose of surveillance and protection, things could still go wrong. I was living proof of that.

When I was a young girl and a teenager up until I was kidnapped, that was the illusion I'd had. That I would always be safe at home. That the Baranov forces would protect me.

They failed to before. When we were taken, the guards had been drugged. A smoke bomb had rendered them unconscious so the kidnappers could swiftly sneak in and take me and my mother.

It happened before and it could again.

Unfortunately for them, whoever dared to cut the power and trespass, I wasn't the kind of person to repeat my mistakes.

I lived and learned.

I'd spent so much time clinging to the fantasy of coming home to be reunited with my family that I never really developed a conviction that I'd be one hundred percent safe here.

I wouldn't be.

And that was why I was prepared to stand here as the eldest Mafia princess. That was why I had the courage to stay steady on my feet and have a gun ready as one of the pregnant women in this small group. It was also why I didn't let the fear or anxiety claim me as I remained tense and listened.

There.

Footsteps sounded outside the hallway. In the stretch of the corridor that connected this great room with the foyer, the sound of softly placed footsteps on the polished marble reached me.

I heard it, straining to keep listening and not lose it. Without turning my head, staying perfectly still, I narrowed my eyes and relied on my senses to lead me.

Again.

Someone was definitely walking in here. An intruder had gotten past the guards to be walking in the house. I hadn't imagined it. I heard it. Someone was definitely sneaking further inside.

Releasing and re-tightening my fingers on the gun, I mentally charged myself to be ready to act. Steeling my spine and steadying my breath, I waited until I could aim and end this danger.

No one stirred on the couch. The other women were just as quiet, and I knew without looking that Eva had to have her gun up.

Then movement entered my vision. As I locked my stare on the open doorway, I watched as an object came into the room.

A slim, dark object flew through the air, dropping on the floor and rolling. The short cylindrical item stopped when it collided against the leg of a side table.

Mist hissed and escaped an opening at the end of it.

Gas.

A stark sense of terrible déjà vu hit me.

It was just like before.

Someone slipping in and using a gas bomb to render the guards unconscious.

The Ilyins? Again?

I clamped my teeth together so tightly that my jaw and teeth ached. Knowing the same assholes who'd taken me before would try to do this again was too much to handle.

"No."

One of the women whispered it, spotting the rising fumes.

Without risking too much movement before the trespasser could see us and know where to fire, I stayed still even as one of the women rushed forward.

Irina. I saw her long hair as she dove forward. With her shirt pulled up over her mouth and nose in a makeshift mask, she lunged down to the floor, grabbed the gas bomb, and ran.

Reaching the windows, she flung one open and lobbed the gas bomb out into the yard. Before she could fully spin and face us in the room again, my mark made himself visible.

"I wouldn't," the Ilyin said neutrally.

He placed one foot, then another. Slowly, he entered my line of sight. He crept closer, hands up, until he was fully in the room.

"I wouldn't shoot," he warned.

Numerous thick packs and devices were strapped on him. Over his chest, his abdomen, and onto his back. As he stepped completely into the room, turning slightly in order to face me, the sobering and horrifying realization of what we were facing dawned on me.

Bombs.

He was covered with bombs. The shapes and wires connecting them were too damn obvious.

And in his hand, raised with his fingers up but his thumb down to hold something in his clutch, was a slim stick with a blue button at the top.

He held the detonator.

"If you shoot, I'll press this button."

My lips trembled under the pressure to kill him. In the face of a direct threat like this, I vibrated with so much anger, I couldn't contain it. Still, I kept my arms locked and ready, the gun firmly in my hands and aimed at his head.

"Do you hear me?" he asked, deferring to me since I was in the front of the room.

"Fuck you," I growled through clenched teeth.

"Don't test me," he warned. "I'll press this button before you can shoot."

I wasn't in any position to guess or wager who would be faster. Maybe he had a quicker reflex and trigger finger. I didn't know. All I could assume was that pressing that button would cause an immediate detonation whereas the bullet I fired at him would have to pass over the distance of this room to reach him.

"I'll be damned if you try to ruin my life again."

He lifted his chin, so loyal to his leader that he would be a kamikaze soldier. If he wasn't here to capture me and the others behind me on the couch, then he had to be here to kill us.

"You won't take me. Not again."

He didn't respond.

"I'm sick of you fucking Ilyins trying to destroy my family. I won't be a pawn you can use in your schemes." With every word I said, the decibel of my voice scaled higher and louder until I was screaming.

"I am devoted to the prosperity of my family," I vowed. "And I order you to leave. Now!"

"Shut the fuck up and sit down."

"No," I bit it out with such vehemence I felt like my blood was boiling and spilling over. "Get out of this house now."

"I'm not listening to a single fucking thing any Baranov bitch says—" He turned his head slightly. Without taking his attention off me, he shifted just a little. Clued in to someone else entering the house, he reacted and registered that we weren't alone.

My stupid heart lifted. I wanted to believe it was help arriving. That Ben and Lev were back. Vik and Rurik. Any of the many loyal guards and soldiers in this organization.

Anything could go wrong on a day like today with so many deadly missions and goals being put into action.

But it looked like *everything* was bound to go wrong on a day like today.

It wasn't any of the Baranov men who rushed in from the front door. It wasn't the man I wanted to call my husband. It wasn't my brother-in-law or cousins.

It was a stranger. With a deranged, maniacal grin morphing his face, he ran in to stand next to the Ilyin strapped with bombs. As he skidded to a stop, surveying the man then the rest of us in the room, he nodded and chuckled. The long black coat he wore dripped water onto the floor, making his shoes squeak with his steps as he walked in further, but beneath it, his suit gave me no clue who he was.

An enemy.

That was all I needed to identify him.

He was an enemy to smile at the sight of bombs in our place. He was an enemy because he held a gun in one hand.

"Just in time." He smiled at the Ilyin, pointing his gun at him. "Give me the detonator."

"Get the fuck out of here," Eva demanded. "Both of you." She'd come to stand next to me, gun up and ready.

"No," the man said. "No, no, no. You're done. You are all done. This is the end of the Baranovs." He waggled his gun at the soldier. "Give me the detonator now. I hurried here to watch the carnage. To see this place blown to rubble. All of you bitches dead. Now I can be the one to press the button. And everyone can know I was the one to end your fucking family once and for all."

The Ilyin handed the detonator to him. His vacant stare proved that he'd accepted his death. In suicide, in the name of serving his family or this stranger. However he justified it in his mind. With a lift of his arm, he moved the detonator closer to this businessman.

But he didn't go far with it.

"Fuck you, O'Malley." Kelly screamed it, coming between me and Eva. "Fuck you!"

She was the one who'd taken that third gun. She was the one who screamed so loudly as she emptied the clip into O'Malley. Whoever he was, she'd gotten him at the perfect moment of distraction. He dropped the detonator at her scream.

Perhaps he hadn't seen her seated behind me and my sister. Maybe it was the feral ferocity of her screams that jarred him and distracted him from holding on to the detonator.

Kelly missed twice, but as she walked forward, elbows locked, both hands on her gun, she ensured that he was directly in her line of fire.

And she shot and shot. Plugging him with one bullet after the next, she sank lead into his chest, his stomach, his neck. They weren't clean shots, but all of them worked to kill him.

Just in case, I lifted my gun to fire once. A clean hole between his eyes would promise he was definitely dead in case her shots didn't work fast enough.

"Get the—" Irina lunged forward again, diving low to grab something off the floor. She wasn't afraid of the violence, not even caring that O'Malley was still falling over and slumping to his death as he stared at Kelly glaring down at him.

The detonator had fallen to the floor from the botched handoff between the bomb-laden soldier and O'Malley.

Irina dipped to get it at the same time the soldier did.

But before either could claim it, the man stood and tried to rip at the bombs, probably intending to sever the wires and set it off just the same.

"What the—"

Gunfire followed the grumbled question to the side of the room. Two shots sounded off, and the Ilyin guard dropped down. His hands didn't move. *He* didn't move with his head blown to bits.

I whipped my head around, finding Uncle Oleg standing in the hallway.

He still blinked his eyes, clearing the sleepy, drowsy look from his face. With his gun still lowering, it was clear he was the one who'd shot him.

Finally, *finally*, I lowered my arms. Releasing a long exhale, I sighed and let all the pent-up stress seep from me at the sight of my uncle, the Boss, standing there and taking charge.

It was over. It had to be over, and as I willed my heart to slow, I tested a new reality on myself.

They were dead.

All of them.

Every one of our most determined enemies were dead or soon would be.

Eva eased Kelly back from O'Malley's body. Uncle Oleg walked further into the room, more alert and concerned. He glanced at me, raising his brows while Irina backed up to help Eva with Kelly, who seemed the most stunned.

I opened my mouth to say something. To tell Uncle Oleg thanks. Or to confirm that we were okay. Something had to be said to snap us further out of this shock.

But I didn't need to. Tires squealed outside and the hammering footsteps of running men came.

"Sonya!"

My lips slightly lifted of their own accord.

Ben.

It was Ben yelling as he ran inside. Lev was right there with him. They didn't stop, still holding their guns as they rushed toward me and Eva.

Only when his arms were wrapped tightly around me did I know everything would be okay.

"Rurik called and said he'd received a notification that the power was cut," Lev said, talking to Oleg.

"He's alive?" Kelly cried out from behind Irina as she hugged her.

Lev nodded.

I stared up at Ben, needing another moment of the comfort he gave me. As they started to talk and collaborate on what had gone down, I closed my eyes to accept Ben's kiss.

Then resting my cheek against his chest, hearing his steady heartbeat, I held on to my future and knew it would be as bright and full as I dreamed it could be.

The danger was over.

For good.

With sacrifices from us all, through teamwork and counting on every one of us surviving our hardships, we removed the danger from our lives so the Baranov legacy would continue into the next generation.

30

BEN

Two months later...

"At least I didn't need to sneak into *this* wedding," I joked as I sat at the table up near where Irina and Vik smiled and kissed again. They were just as sappy and happy newlyweds as Eva and Lev had been back in the spring.

"Stop," Sonya chided playfully, swatting at my thigh.

Lev rolled his eyes, seated next to me with Eva.

"Which one was better?" Eva asked. It seemed that she'd gotten the most addicted to the whole wedding planning part of the Baranov family.

"What?" I huffed. "I don't know."

Sonya shifted on her seat, comfortable since she hadn't even tried to wear heels. In a pink gown that gave room for her belly, she looked beautiful on this July evening too. She'd be gorgeous no matter what she wore—or didn't—and I wondered how I'd ever gotten so lucky to have a woman who got even more alluring when she was carrying a baby.

Our baby.

Every time I reminded myself that I'd be a father soon, I was struck with the pure marvel and awe that it was coming true. That I wasn't lost or solo. I would have a son or daughter soon. Smiling at her, I nestled her close and rested my hand on her belly, possessive as ever.

"I'm still sad I didn't get to see your wedding," Sonya said. She was honest with her comment, but the sadness in her tone wasn't as heavy as it was a month or two ago.

After we confirmed all our enemies were dead—Benson, O'Malley, the Petrovs, and even the Ilyins, whom Vik and Rurik slayed that one day—we all had our own traumas to move past.

Sonya was brave and strong, toughing it out the best she could. It was only in the last couple of weeks that she'd stopped waking from night terrors. It was only recently that she'd gotten to a place where she could avoid locking into a depressed, vacant state of mind and live in the moment.

Eleven years of captivity weren't something anyone could recover from in a short time. The other horrors she'd witnessed and endured compounded the demons in her head.

"Then you'll get to see it when we renew our vows," Eva said. "And it was just one day. One party. One wedding. You are here, and you're not leaving, and you can see our marriage play out. That matters so much more than one wedding." She placed her hand on Sonya's and the sisters smiled.

"I know," Sonya said with a sigh.

I rubbed her shoulder so she could rest her head on me.

"But which one was better?" Eva asked me again.

I rolled my eyes as we all laughed. "Um, this one?"

She mocked disgust at my answer, pretending to be offended. "What? No."

"Well, so far, no one has keeled over and died at this one."

They all shot me wry, dirty looks.

Okay. I guess this isn't an opportune time for any dark humor...

I smiled quickly. "Just kidding."

"Don't jinx it," Lev warned with another side eye.

Sonya grunted. "Jinx it? Come on. You can't buy into that superstition crap. You believe in jinxes?"

"No," Lev replied. "It's just a saying. After all the shit we've gone through recently, let's not borrow any trouble from the potential that jinxes can be real."

I shook my head, sighing happily with my woman at my side. "But that's just it. After all the shit we've gone through recently, what else could possibly go wrong now?"

Everyone who could hurt this family was dead, wounded, or gone. Both politicians were six feet under. The Petrovs were so weakened and scrambling without a leader that they practically ceased to exist as an organization. After Irina killed Igor, and since she was planning to marry into the Baranovs today, there was no one to guide the fractured family. Infighting didn't help, and it was with confidence that all of us could know the Petrovs were done.

Vik and Rurik had eliminated the Ilyins, too. Some members might still be out there, but so few were left that it would take them at least an entire generation or two to get back to any status of power that they'd once had. Finding the family members at a big meeting made Vik and Rurik's job of annihilating the family in one attack all too easy.

"There will always be another danger lurking," Oleg said.

I nodded, respecting the Boss's opinion. And of course, he was right. Danger was a constant in the Mafia way of life.

But for now, I was content with the relative peace.

"Lev, a word," Oleg said as he got up from the table. With a tip of his head toward the side, he indicated for Lev to follow him.

It had to be another discussion about business. More and more, since that fateful day we'd almost lost our women, he'd been taking up a role of being the next boss. Oleg was slowly but surely training Lev to be the next leader of the family. If it wasn't due to his heart attack and health scare, his desire to step down had to be due to his desire to spoil all the babies coming into the world soon.

And I was glad to leave it to him. Lev could be the boss. I'd heed his word, too. Being one of the brothers, lateral to Vik and Rurik, was just fine for me. I'd meant it when I said I wanted to focus on my family.

Which was why I asked Sonya to get up with me. "If you'll excuse me, I'd like to dance with this gorgeous creature again."

Sonya smiled slyly, amused, and came onto the dance floor with me. "Beautiful *creature*? I'm not even a woman anymore?"

Facing her as I gathered her close, as close as I could with our baby in between us, I smiled easily. "A ravishing creature."

"More animal than person." She groaned slightly, lifting her feet one at a time. "With how I waddle like a penguin, and this big old belly making me look like a whale."

I kissed her, loving her with all my heart as she shared her self-deprecation with humor. Her smile had yet to vanish.

"Nonsense. All I see is the lovely mother of my children."

"Children?" She laughed once. "How about we just go with one for now?"

"I'll go with whatever you want," I said. "One. Two. Ten."

"Ten!" She laughed freely, making me wish she'd never stop being this carefree. "I'm not agreeing to ten. But I would love to have more. Maybe we can pace them out, is all."

"Whatever you want," I promised.

"Maybe five," she amended with a shrug.

"Deal."

"No, six. An even number would be easier."

"How so?"

"I don't know. But seven sounds like too many and five doesn't sound like enough."

I laughed, kissing her again as my chuckles faded. "We'll figure it out." I was overjoyed she was on the same page as me, though. She was interested in having more kids despite her discomfort with this pregnancy as it progressed. She was determined to start a big family. It was my biggest dream coming true, finding my one true love and settling down with her for the rest of my life.

But first...

"And I don't think every day for the rest of my life with you will ever be enough either," I said. "I love you, Sonya."

She smiled so sweetly, gazing up at me with that tender stare. "I love you, too."

"Maybe you had to miss Eva's wedding." I reached into my pocket for a ring I'd spent days deliberating over. Lev, Vik, Rurik, Oleg, and even Maxim helped me pick it. I would never doubt how much I was included in this family. As I presented it to her, I admired the sparkle of glee in her eyes. "But Eva won't have to miss yours."

She sniffled once, prone to tears with the hormones controlling her. These were happy tears, though. Her grin couldn't stretch any wider.

"Will you marry me, Sonya? Will you be my wife?"

Nodding quickly, almost jerkily with how overcome she was by emotions, she laughed. "Yes. Yes, Ben. I can't wait to be your wife."

I kissed her hard, loving the press of her smile against my lips.

31

SONYA

Three months later...

I clenched my teeth, bearing through the pain that I was supposed to be able to handle as a woman.

Life was no easy adventure. It hadn't been so far. As a Mafia princess, like my sister and friends, I would always be held to the expectation to tough out more than any ordinary woman could face.

Being kidnapped.

Watching my mother raped and killed.

Threats of rape.

Fighting off killers.

Facing deadly men who wanted to threaten my family.

But this…

"Come on, Sonya. You're doing fine," Ben promised. He clutched my hand, holding it tight.

"I am *not* doing fine!" I snapped, biting out the word through clenched teeth.

Giving birth was hands-down the hardest thing I'd ever experienced in my life.

"I don't want you to gaslight me. I am *not* doing fine. I feel like I'm being ripped apart and splintered and—" Another scream tore from my lips. I roared, baring my teeth and trying to stay awake through the agony of pushing my baby out.

"You *are* doing fine," Irina coached. She was here too, the most experienced and hence the one I wanted in the room with Ben. Once an enemy but now a cousin, she was a close confidante I couldn't imagine not having in my second take on life. She'd given birth a couple of weeks ago. Regardless of all the complications she'd faced, she and her son were healthy and whole. It was her expertise and recent experience of advocating for herself during her childbirth experience that made me want her near.

"You're almost there."

"It doesn't seem like it," I protested, breathing hard.

"Well, after thirty hours of labor, I bet not," she replied, almost teasing. "But you are doing fine. You and the baby are doing fine. No concerns. It just hurts."

"A lot," I agreed as another contraction came.

Eva was in another room, being monitored for her pregnancy. After the misfortune of a miscarriage, she quickly found out she was pregnant with twins. And with more cramps and spotting, she was already on bedrest and monitored.

I wanted to be there for her. That was how much I cared about my family at all times, no matter what. Nothing would ever complicate or end my devotion to my family.

"One more push, Sonya," the doctor said.

I closed my eyes, feeling Ben's fingers gripping my hand tighter. Bearing down, I tried to do as the doctor said. I tried. I fought. I persisted through the agony claiming my body, mind, and soul.

And it was over.

I sucked in a breath, fearing I would throw up. But the pressure was gone. The sharp pain receded—not disappearing, but changing.

I no longer felt like I was being stretched and ripped in half.

And as I blinked and opened my eyes to the sensation of Ben's lips on my temple, I heard it.

A cry.

A single cry.

Tears streamed down my cheeks. I couldn't stem the flow. Something intrinsic in me snapped into place. Hearing my baby's cry for the first time was a moment I would never, ever forget.

Smiling in relief and laughing at the miracle of life, I opened my eyes to the precious baby the doctors wrapped up and held high.

"You did it," Ben said. He kissed me again. "I love you. I love you so much. You did it."

I laughed again, almost lightheaded and hysterical coming down from that experience. "We did it. We did *that*. We had that." I pointed weakly at the baby.

Irina brushed my hair back, also crying happy tears as she stood by and held my other hand.

"Oh, my God," Eva said.

Even though she wasn't here, because we were Baranovs and nothing was impossible, we got our way to have her "watching" via a FaceTime call. She couldn't be in the room with me, but Irina sat a phone to the side so she'd be here remotely.

"Sonya." Eva sobbed happily. "Oh, Sonya."

I laughed again, my heart so full it would burst. "We did it," I told Ben, gazing up at him with so much love. I was overcome by so many emotions and feelings that I couldn't keep up. I couldn't react or focus on anything but the new life the doctor brought to me.

"No more *it* or *that*," Irina said.

I accepted my baby as the doctor placed him or her on my chest.

"A girl," she announced with a proud smile. "You did it, Sonya. You are amazing. The longest labor I'd ever witnessed." She looked at her watch and laughed once. "Just past midnight."

I cried a little more, looking at the face of my sweet baby girl.

Ben leaned over, hugging me as we both admired our first daughter. As hellish as giving birth was, I would never pass up on experiencing this miracle again.

"Jennifer," I said softly, "welcome to the world."

Ben kissed my brow again.

"Your mommy and daddy already love you, Jenny." I drew in a deep breath, confident that naming her after the brave woman who'd shown me compassion in my escape was the right thing to do.

Ben and Oleg delivered my letter to the Petersons, and I had no doubt they'd upped the deposit of money I wanted them to give. Mere thanks weren't enough. I would be eternally grateful for their compassion toward me when I needed it the most.

"She's beautiful," Irina said.

"Henry's going to have his cousin to grow up with now, a boy and a girl. That'll keep us busy," I said, gazing at every little wrinkle of her pink face.

"Until Kelly's boy or girl is here," Ben said.

"Then add two more!" Eva said from the phone.

Irina reached over to bring the phone over. She probably had only heard it all, but now she could see.

"Oh, Sonya." She cried, happy tears leaking down her face. "She's precious."

"I love you, Sis," I replied.

"I love you, too."

It meant the world to me that I could share this experience with her. And it mattered deep down in my soul that I'd made this happen.

I took the chances to escape. I'd taken the step to reclaim control in my life to avoid being presented as a forced virginal bride to Eric Benson.

I never could have anticipated that in doing so, I was starting my family and future.

Vik knocked on the door, entering to join Irina. "How's it—oh!" He grinned, walking closer but not nearing the foot of my bed as the nurses finished with me. "He or she is here!"

"After what the doctor confirmed was the longest labor she'd ever witnessed in her career," Ben said.

He winced playfully and smiled at me. "Congratulations. Should I tell Oleg that Henry's got a boy or a girl to chase around at home now?"

Oleg was at home with Rurik and Kelly, waiting for the news.

"Vik, meet Jenny," I said.

"No man is ever going to be good enough for you, little girl," he said.

I rolled my eyes.

Ben laughed, shaking his head.

"I guess I owe Lev a hundred," Vik joked, shoving his hands in his pockets.

"You bet on our kid?" Ben said.

"Ah, just guessing the gender." Vik winked. "Since no one wants to find out the gender beforehand."

"Nope." I smiled wider. "I like wondering."

"But it would make it easier to decorate," Irina said. They hadn't learned the gender ahead of time, either. Like Ben and me, they were moving into their new house. As far as I could tell, they hadn't struggled with decorating their nursery. And I bet we'd all be accessorizing and decorating after the fact as we welcomed our babies home.

"I'm not finding out either," Eva said on the phone. "But I'll put a hundred on it being two girls."

I laughed. "Two girls?"

"Yeah. Sisters. They'd always have each other like we did."

A poignant stab of hurt made my heart ache. *Like we did?* We were separated for eleven years. And she'd gotten stuck on the fear and assumption that I'd willingly run away.

I dismissed the reminder, though. I couldn't let my past trauma trap me in sadness or anger.

It was time to look forward, to embrace each new day as it came and anticipate all the things that the next day could bring too.

And I wouldn't do it alone. I had my fiancé—the one I chose and would pick time and time again. I had my daughter. My uncle. My cousins and their spouses and a whole new generation of Baranovs on their way.

"Sisters," I agreed with Eva, meeting her eyes on the screen. "Together forever."

From this day on.

She sniffled, smiling back at me.

We would all be together, no matter the trials and threats. No matter the danger and enemies, that was who we were. The Baranovs weren't just an organization. We were family. We would uphold our legacy with love and determination to always support each other.

I looked around the room, appreciating that they were all here.

That Ben was here to show me how to let the love and trust in.

Meeting his eyes, I sighed and mouthed, *I love you*, knowing I was free to do so for the rest of my days.

Printed in Great Britain
by Amazon